ALABAMA RAIDER

HARVE STEIN

ALABAMA RAIDER

By BETTY BAXTER ANDERSON

Illustrated by Harve Stein

The John C. Winston Company
Philadelphia · Toronto

First Edition

Made in the United States of America
L.C. Card # 57-10193

About the Author

Photographs and a collection of 19th century magazines started Betty Baxter Anderson writing her first book about the War Between the States. A few years ago when Mrs. Anderson inherited a photographic history of the War Between the States and ten bound volumes of *Harper's Illustrated Weekly,* dating from 1861-1870, she became so absorbed that she has added more than a hundred books covering this period to her library, concentrating on those dealing with the Navy. ALABAMA RAIDER is the result of her thoughtful research. She was originally attracted to the story of the *Alabama* because of the unusual facts that surrounded the ship's launching and which started the vessel on her short but dazzling career.

Mrs. Anderson was born in Benton, Iowa. She graduated from the University of Iowa School of Journalism. She has worked as a newspaper writer, but her real medium is juvenile fiction; she has written seventeen books ranging in subject matter from farm life to mysteries and historical incidents.

Now living in La Jolla, California, with her husband and two children, Mrs. Anderson is hopeful that ALABAMA RAIDER will illuminate that which has been a relatively little-known aspect of the Confederate Navy's battles during the war.

With the exceptions of Midshipmen Timothy Moore and Clint Stokes, the characters of ALABAMA RAIDER are historical. For obvious reasons, the paymaster has been given a fictitious name.

B. B. A.

Contents

Chapter 1

SATCHEL OF GOLD

THE door marked "Bureau of Provisions and Clothing" suddenly swung open and a page announced, "Midshipman Moore! Secretary Mallory wants you to report at once."

"Secretary Mallory wants to *see me?*" Tim's voice, in spite of his height of 6 feet and new beard, still had a trick of going off into a treble. However none of the other young officers at nearby desks laughed, for it was a solemn occasion when the Secretary of the Confederate Navy sent for a man.

Timothy Moore made no attempt to gather the papers scattered on his desk, but jumped to obey orders.

As he followed the page down the hall he swiftly buttoned his gray jacket. In late June, in Richmond, the morning heat was stifling.

The young officer wasn't kept in suspense long. Stephen Russell Mallory was a man of action. "Sit down, Mr. Moore," he said with a smile. "Be with you in a moment."

During the time he had served in the Confederate

Navy headquarters, Tim had seen the Secretary often, but he'd never had the chance to study him this closely before.

He saw a strong, chunky man, whose short hair and closely trimmed beard exaggerated the square lines of his face. He had a generous mouth and lively blue eyes.

"Mr. Moore, when you resigned your commission in the Union Navy last year, did you think you were going to see action right away for your state?"

The question was unexpected, but Tim replied quickly. "Yes, sir. The day after Virginia seceded I volunteered for duty with you."

"You didn't expect you'd be serving for more than a year over a desk, did you?"

"No, sir."

The older man chuckled. "Well, I've had good reports about your devotion to dull duty. Mr. Moore, would you like an exciting and responsible task, even if it involved danger?"

"Yes, sir!"

Secretary Mallory opened a deep drawer of his desk and produced a battered satchel. "Under a false bottom of this case is a great deal of gold," he said. "I'm not going to tell you how much, but its delivery into the right hands is important." He gave the tall midshipman a keen glance. "You've heard of the *290,* of course?"

"Yes, Mr. Mallory." Tim made no attempt to hide his delight. "You mean—you want me to take that satchel to England?"

The older man was serious as he leafed through the telegrams on his desk. "Word has come to us from Captain Bulloch in England that we must get the *290* to sea as soon as possible. Captain Raphael Semmes is to command, and we have sent his orders to Nassau to turn him around and get him back to England." He gave Tim another searching look. "I needn't add that all this is in the strictest confidence. That is why I am giving you verbal orders.

"Great Britain has announced her neutrality, but the Confederate States have powerful friends there. Unfortunately, our enemies have influence, too, and it looks as if England may shortly render an opinion against us. If that government decides the vessel is intended for 'warlike use,' the officers of the Crown may seize her before she leaves the Lairds' docks.

"You will not go back to your desk, but go to your rooming house at once and pack. You'll leave from the Byrd Street Station of the Richmond & Petersburg Railroad this afternoon for Charleston. Go on board the *New Dolphin* at once; the captain expects you. You may put the satchel in his safe until you reach Liverpool. Until it is in that safe, however, be sure to keep it in sight every second."

He paused and added slowly, *"Once in England, don't let it out of your hands until you turn it over to Captain Semmes."*

"Aye, aye, sir."

"From that time on," Secretary Mallory continued,

"your orders are written. You are to sail with the *290,* or as she will be commissioned, the *Alabama.*"

Only his years of discipline at Annapolis and his more recent duty with the Confederate Navy kept Midshipman Moore from giving the famous Rebel yell.

At last he was going to sea! Every one of the 332 officers who had resigned from the United States Navy to serve the Confederacy would have been proud and happy to have this opportunity. Yet only twenty could have the honor of serving aboard the sleek new cruiser.

"Thank you, sir."

"Now, you'd better get on. Along with your orders in this envelope is the money for your traveling expenses. If you'd like to send some notes to your family and closest friends, mail them from Charleston. Just tell them you are going on a government mission and not to be alarmed if they don't hear from you for several weeks."

"It will be easier than having to say good-by."

Secretary Mallory stood up and extended his hand. "I only wish I could go along. Good luck."

Once on the steamcars, the precious satchel concealed within his own larger traveling case beside him on the seat, Tim had time to consider the amazing events of the day. He gazed intently out his window at the green countryside as the train rolled along at 10 miles an hour. He wondered how many months would pass before he saw the familiar landscape again.

Last year it had been a hard decision to leave the

Naval Academy and his friends, but Tim felt strongly that he owed his allegiance to his native state. When Virginia left the Union, he left, too, filled with zeal and enthusiasm for the task ahead.

The South, for all its many loyal and able Navy men, had practically no ships. It lacked steel mills, raw materials and mechanical building experience.

Great hopes were based on Capt. James Bulloch, who had been sent to England with gold and credits to have Confederate raiders built.

President Jefferson Davis had issued letters of marque to privately owned vessels to seize and raid Union merchant ships. Then France and England had decided to maintain a strict neutrality. Other countries followed their lead, and the privateers had no place to sell their captures for prize money.

Still, the few Confederate warships could and did destroy all the Union shipping they could trap.

Tim fought to keep himself awake through the night. The soft, Southern voices of the other passengers were reassuring, but anyone could be a traitor or a spy or a thief.

Only once during the trip did Tim leave his seat, and then he lugged his big, heavy case with him. The train stopped for a half hour at a dingy station so that the passengers could buy refreshments. Tim drank two mugs of black coffee and ate a thick beef sandwich. Afterward, it was easier to keep awake.

Wonder if any of my friends from Annapolis will be

in England? Tim thought. I know Maffitt and Anderson were on the *Sumter,* the lucky dogs. We've certainly scattered. Doubt if I'll ever see the ones who went over to the Yankees. He squirmed uncomfortably at the next thought.

Now that I'm really going on board a warship, I may be shooting at some of them. Lots of them weren't good friends because that last year we were already choosing sides. Tim chuckled a bit at the memory of some of the hottest debates. Good thing the Navy's so strict about duels and fights or there might not be any midshipmen left. Still, there were a few who stayed out of the arguments. I was surprised at Baird and Stokes going with the Yankees. The Confederacy suffered no great loss there. Stokes, for sure, always tried to get the soft jobs.

When the train finally reached Charleston, Tim was almost staggering with weariness.

Captain Benton of the *New Dolphin* was a bluff, hearty man. "Glad to see you, my boy! We may get off tonight. It's the dark of the moon and easy enough to give those blockheaded blockaders the slip."

Tim nodded, too tired to smile.

"I can see you're about to drop in your tracks. Want some warm food or a hot berth, first?" His laugh boomed.

"I'd like to stow my satchel in your safe, sir. Then I'd like that berth. Never thought I'd ever be more sleepy than hungry."

Tim saw the satchel locked in the big iron safe, then

followed the captain across the wardroom to the passenger cabins.

Next morning, Tim was aroused by a knock. Still groggy with sleep, he opened the door to admit the steward, bearing a linen-covered tray.

"Are we at sea?"

The colored man chuckled. "Yassuh!" He whisked the napkin off the tray to reveal a pot of coffee, a dish of applesauce, fried ham, eggs and biscuits. "Them old warships didn't even know we'd moved. Run right out under their noses and we've been under sail about 4 hours. Cap'n Benton, he's afraid you goin' to waste away iffen you don't get some food."

"You come back in 10 minutes and you won't see a crumb left on that tray."

The blockade runner *New Dolphin,* hold full of tobacco, sailed serenely for England. Tim, relieved of the responsibility of the gold, enjoyed every minute.

The trip was smooth and the young midshipman utilized his time by reviewing his knowledge of navigating by sun and stars, and practicing heaving lines, tying knots and splicing. After more than a year of clerking in an office, it was thrilling for him to breathe salt air and refresh his nautical skills.

Once in England, the weight of the gold he carried felt to Tim as if he had the whole world on his shoulders.

A few hours after he'd said good-by to Captain Benton in Liverpool, Tim was at Birkenhead.

He stood on the dock and gazed in delight for a few minutes at the bark-rigged vessel which had been pointed out to him as the *290*. The sleek craft was known by that number, since she was the two-hundred-ninetieth ship built by the Lairds.

Familiar with her statistics from his work in the Confederate Navy headquarters, he checked his memory. The vessel was slightly over 1,000 tons' register, 210 feet long, with a 32-foot beam. There were 2 horizontal engines, each of 300 horsepower, with stowage for 350 tons of coal.

Still admiring her, Tim walked toward the gangplank. She looked seaworthy, gleaming with paint and with sails neatly furled. Workmen hurried about with tools, ropes, planks.

A couple of tough-looking guards stepped toward him. "Your business here, sir?"

Tim halted. "I'm Mid. Timothy Moore from Virginia, reporting to Captain Semmes."

"Captain Semmes has not arrived."

Tim was shocked. What should he do now?

He could hear Secretary Mallory's voice in firm echo. "Once in England, don't let the gold out of your hands until you turn it over to Captain Semmes." The valise seemed pounds heavier.

After a moment's hesitation, Tim asked, "Where can I find Captain Bulloch? Capt. James Bulloch?"

"He's aboard; we'll take word to him. Midshipman Moore from Virginia?"

Tim nodded eagerly. "From Confederate Navy headquarters in Richmond."

A moment later, one of the guards signaled. Tim raced up the gangplank. He was looking forward to meeting Captain Bulloch, a Georgian who had been trained in the old Navy, but who had retired some years before the war. Since secession, he had been working hard for the Confederacy, acquiring ships in England.

The officers' wardroom was first-class, Tim noted happily as he followed the guard. Then he was shaking hands with Captain Bulloch.

"So you're from Richmond, eh?"

"Yes, sir. I'm on a mission from Secretary Mallory to Captain Semmes." He grinned. "I have orders to the *Alabama*."

Captain Bulloch returned the grin. "For a few more days it will be *290*. I am sorry to tell you that Captain Semmes isn't here yet."

He nodded toward the calendar on the desk. "We have it on good authority that the Crown has rendered an adverse opinion. We are to be seized in a day or two. Legally, we're clear, since we have no guns, no ammunition, no officers or crew. The delay, however, would be disastrous."

Amazingly, after this bad news, Captain Bulloch chuckled. "Tomorrow, the builders are having a trial run. A number of friends, the custom officials and some charming ladies are coming aboard; just a little picnic feast and celebration."

Tim was puzzled. A picnic on this fine warship?

Captain Bulloch went on. "You'll want to stay on board. Midshipmen will be berthed in the starboard steerage, but you'll have it to yourself for the time being."

Still clutching the heavy satchel, Tim followed a steward whom Captain Bulloch had ordered to show the way.

Within an hour, Tim had stowed his gear and made up his berth. On deck there were the noises of hammering, sawing, men shouting. He had never felt so alone and so strange in all his life.

Wearily, he took the battered satchel from his traveling case and put it on the bunk. He dozed, his head resting on the awkward pillow, both hands clenched on the handle.

Tim woke after dark, unaware that Captain Bulloch had gone ashore in the meantime. The cruiser was quiet now; he was still alone in his quarters and decided that he might as well sleep.

He was startled awake next morning by the throb of the engines. The satchel was still safe, under his head. He rose and stretched.

Over the sound of the engines he could hear voices. Gay, laughing, feminine voices! Tim glanced up the hatch and saw a group of stylishly dressed women coming up the gangplank. There were quite a few men, too, carrying wicker picnic baskets.

"What a way to go to sea on a cruiser in wartime!" Tim muttered. With a sigh, he picked up the satchel.

He'd go to the wardroom and try to rustle some breakfast.

A steward brought Tim coffee, fruit and a roll. There were no officers about so, feeling disconsolate, he went back to his quarters.

The engines began to turn faster. To the cheers of watchers on the dock, the sleek new vessel slid off into the tide-ripped waters of the River Mersey.

The cheerful voices from the deck only added to Tim's gloom. Might as well be back at his desk in Richmond, for all the good this was going to do for the Confederacy. A Sunday picnic on a river!

Tim glared at the scarred leather case on his berth. He could see weeks of carrying it around, day and night, while the courts of England deliberated the fate of the *290*.

Tim had no idea how long it had been since leaving the dock when the engines slowed, then stopped abruptly. He leaped to look up the hatch.

A tug had come alongside the vessel and the visitors were leaving! Tim looked back across the shimmering water toward land, and pounded the satchel in joy.

"Jiminy!" he shouted to his weighty old companion. "We've really gone to sea. The Crown can't stop us now. We're outside the marine limits!"

Chapter 2

CLASSMATES

CAPTAIN BUTCHER, the English commander, was briskly issuing orders to his skeleton staff of a half-dozen British officers, when Tim rushed up on deck lugging his clumsy burden.

"I can see you are undermanned, sir, and I'd like to help," Tim said, when he'd caught the captain's attention. "Only thing is, I have to keep this satchel in my own hands until I turn it over to Captain Semmes."

Captain Butcher said, "That will be at least a fortnight, Mr. Moore. If you're going to be of any use—and we do need you—you'll have to stow it somewhere. There's a strongbox in my cabin."

"Good! Seems as if I've been toting this blamed thing for months."

"The barometer's dropping. We're going to have a rough trip. Come along to my cabin."

Tim could scarcely realize that vile weather was brewing, because the day was warm, bright and sunny. However, by the time he'd locked the satchel in the captain's strongbox and changed to a work uniform, the wind was whipping from the northeast.

Soon the gales were bringing gusts of rain and heavy seas were rolling over the decks. Already on short sail, Captain Butcher ordered the sailors aloft to take close reefs in the topsails, tying them down to about one-third their original size.

Tim gloried in the fresh salt air, the excitement of preparing this new vessel for her first storm. He made himself useful in a dozen ways. Not waiting for orders, he helped pass additional lashings around the quarter-boats after they'd been swung in. Then he volunteered as messenger between the captain on the bridge and the scurrying officers and men on deck.

Captain Butcher, drinking hot tea which Tim had brought to him from the galley, told of the planned rendezvous.

"The *Agrippina,* a sailing ship, left Liverpool with provisions, 250 tons of coal, the battery and ammunition several days ago, headed for Porto Praya. That's on Terceira Island, one of the Azores. She should be there, ready and waiting for us, unless she's run into this same foul weather.

"Captain Semmes is due in London at any time from the Bahamas, and most of his officers are waiting in England or are coming with him."

"Then we'll start raiding in a couple of weeks?" Tim asked.

"We start transferring the stores from the supply

ship as soon as we reach the rendezvous." His voice was cool, a little amused.

Tim blushed. He realized it was not a proper question to ask the British officer. "Is there any danger of trouble with Portugal, using that port?"

Captain Butcher shrugged. "Legally, this is still an English ship with English officers and crew. If any Union warship were to pursue and attack, Portugal as a neutral would be honorbound to stop her. Her defenses, however, are pretty feeble."

The captain paused, and then laughed. "I say, we'll face that one when we come to it. Right now, we've got to keep an eye on the barometer; it's still dropping. There might have to be double watches for all hands."

It was the last chance for conversation that howling, black night. The rain drove relentlessly. The ship fought on around the rugged north coast of Ireland. Tim, when he had time to think, was proud he had his sea legs. Even some of the old salts who had been on land for a time were seasick.

One night, a week out, the fury of the storm seemed spent, and Captain Butcher gave the order to let the steam drop and to raise the propeller.

Tim, curious about this operation he'd never seen, joined a group of sailors watching the propeller being detached from the shaft and lifted to a well built for the purpose. Sam Storr, an ancient, grizzled sailor, said, "Trim a ship as ever I sailed on. Ain't never seen a thing like that afore. No drag from the propeller when we're under canvas, and a good thing. Coal's half gone and another week of this bluster and we'd be in real trouble."

Tim glanced up proudly at the taut canvas above. "Anyway, one good thing about having to run the engines so long. We have plenty of water." He turned to the scuttlebutt for a drink before turning in. The auxiliary machinery included evaporators which supplied the crew with drinking water.

Tim was too busy to keep track of the days and nights, and it was almost 2 weeks before the welcome cry of "Land ho!" came from the lookout on the mast.

The island looked hazy and indistinct at first, but after another hour's brisk sailing, the white houses dotting the mountainsides gleamed in the sun.

Captain Butcher allowed the men no relaxation. By nightfall, the waiting supply ship was lashed alongside the *290,* and the first barrels of beef and pork and the boxes and bales of paymaster's, boatswain's and gunner's stores were stacked on the deck of the new vessel.

The work went on unceasingly for 4 days, while an alert watch was maintained for ships. No one dared discuss the constant dread of being discovered by the enemy. The *290* would be helpless against attack.

Tim had the deck watch just before noon on August 20. He sighted a sail, low on the horizon to starboard. Immediately, he sent a messenger below to inform the captain.

Captain Butcher came on deck with his glass. For

long, anxious moments Tim waited before the older man reported, "It's no man-of-war. It must be the *Bahama,* with Captain Semmes."

Porto Praya was open to the eastward and the wind was quickening from that direction. The heaviest guns were yet to be transshipped. It was impossible to tackle that job in such treacherous seas.

The signal came from Captain Semmes' vessel to follow. The *290* and the *Agrippina* upped anchors and trailed the *Bahama* to Angra Bay on the west side of the island, where the waters were quiet and less dangerous.

This was an easy sail and Tim stood alongside Sam Storr at the rail, watching the other ships. The grizzled, gray-bearded old sailor asked, "What kind of feller is this Semmes?"

"I've never seen him," Tim said, "but even the Yankees know all about him. Soon after the war started he took a little converted steamer, called the *Sumter,* right through the Yankees' blockade at New Orleans and made seventeen captures before he had to lay up in Spain for repairs.

"Three Union warships trapped him in port and bottled him up from January to April. Finally he sold the *Sumter* and his officers went with him a roundabout way to Nassau, where he got his orders to come back and take command of the *Alabama.*" Tim unconsciously straightened and his voice deepened. "I consider it the greatest honor of my life to be able to serve our beloved cause under such a fine leader."

Sam's eyes were twinkling at the young man's earnest tone, but he merely said, "Sounds like quite a feller. Might sign up with him, myself."

Tim, pleased at the prospect of being relieved of the responsibility of the gold, nevertheless was rueful as he surveyed the cluttered, crowded deck of his ship. The crew was a rough mob of oddly dressed seamen, their faces streaked with coal dust and grime. Even the weary officers were unshaven and carelessly dressed.

Captain Butcher shuttled from vessel to vessel, accompanied by a small man in civilian clothes. When they came on board the cruiser, Tim was astonished to hear the British captain address him as Captain Semmes!

It wasn't until 4 o'clock that afternoon that the famous Confederate commander, impressive now in full uniform, came on board to relieve Captain Butcher.

Tim approached. "Midshipman Moore reporting, sir. I have an assignment of gold for you, sent by Secretary Mallory."

"Good. Good. I was able to get a supply through our agents in London, Messrs. Fraser, Trenholm & Company, but an additional sum is most welcome, Mr. Moore."

Tim grinned happily. He was pleased he'd taken

time to trim his beard and change to a fresh uniform. "Also, I should like to report for duty with you, sir. Secretary Mallory sent along my written orders."

Captain Semmes was a quiet, reserved man who smiled and laughed rarely. When he smiled, as now, it was with genuine warmth. "That is excellent news, Mr. Moore. I have a fine group of loyal officers, and you will meet them in the wardroom at dinner in 1 hour."

"I should like to turn the gold over to you now, sir, if I may. It's in the strongbox in your cabin."

Captain Semmes nodded and led the way.

His cabin was a semicircular room in the stern, with a fine horsehair sofa and a horseshoe-shaped table. Tim sighed with relief as he saw the battered satchel in the captain's hands.

Tim was lighthearted, later, as he reported to the wardroom mess. There he was greeted noisily by two midshipmen who had arrived with Captain Semmes. They were his former classmates at Annapolis, Eugene Maffitt and E. M. Anderson, whom he hadn't seen for more than a year.

"Anderson, we've both grown a foot since we saw each other last!"

"Only 8 inches for me. I'm through now; old enough." Midshipman Anderson was more mature looking than his two friends. He had straight, dark brows and wore his hair cut shorter than was the fashion.

Eugene Maffitt chuckled as he shook hands with Tim. "Both of you beat me. I stopped growing while I was still at Annapolis." He was a handsome, cheerful young man, proud of his dark, wavy hair and stylish sideburns.

Another old friend of Tim's, Arthur Sinclair, would serve as fourth lieutenant on the new cruiser.

Many of the others had distinguished themselves in the Confederate States Navy. John McIntosh Kell, first lieutenant and executive officer, gave an instant impression of strength and reliability.

Lieutenants Richard F. Armstrong and Joseph D. Wilson, graduates of the Academy, had been pro-

moted for their work on the *Sumter*. The surgeon, Dr. Francis L. Galt, had also served on that ship. Lieutenant Becker K. Howell, marine officer and a quiet, efficient man, was a brother-in-law of President Jefferson Davis.

Tim was beaming with pride as he acknowledged introductions. It was an honor to be part of such an illustrious group.

To add to his happiness, these men made him the center of attention, eagerly asking questions about the "picnic" ruse.

"The English papers were full of it," Lieutenant Armstrong declared. "That poor old Mr. Charles Francis Adams has just been jumping up and down in a rage ever since. Wager he's blamed near shook that Union Embassy into splinters."

"Tim, you always were the luckiest one," Midshipman Anderson added. "Nothing happened to us; just day after day of poking around in London, waiting."

Basking in their envy and admiration, Tim failed to admit he had been as startled as Mr. Adams when the *290* sailed beyond the marine limit. "Didn't have too much time to think of the excitement," he replied. "It was a rough trip and double watches all the way—"

A sturdy and swarthy midshipman sauntered in. Tim stared in astonishment. "Clint Stokes! I thought you went over to the Yankees!"

Swift anger flashed in the dark eyes, but the reply was a cool drawl. "Now, that's no way to greet an old classmate, Tim Moore. I've been on the *Sumter*. Where have you been?"

Tim flushed. The question sounded innocent, but the taunt was unmistakable. "I've been at headquarters in Richmond," he explained hastily. He went on to add he was glad Clint had joined the Confederate forces. "I heard you'd gone home to St. Louis."

"So I did," Clint replied, unsmiling. "It wasn't much of a trick to get through the lines a year ago. I joined up with Captain Semmes in New Orleans. Hope you didn't gab that crazy story I'd joined the Yanks all over Virginia."

Chapter 3

SHOTS IN THE NIGHT

SEVERAL older officers came in and Tim was introduced. Rodell Carney, the paymaster, was a smooth-mannered gentleman, who acknowledged the introduction with a slight nod and then said, "Dr. Galt, I have some serious matters to discuss with you. I am sure these young gentlemen will excuse us."

Without waiting for a reply, he drew the surgeon into a corner, talking in a low tone.

Tim felt as if he'd had cold water dashed in his face. The group became stiff and formal. Talk concerned only the trial cruises to get the *290* in battle condition.

Tim's moment of glory, of warm and admiring companionship, was all too brief. He bitterly resented the abrupt deflation of his self-importance that Rodell Carney had managed so quickly and so easily.

Even when he tried to recapture a little of that glory later, when he and the other young officers returned to their quarters, he was disappointed. He started to describe the storms encountered on the trip to the Azores when Anderson yawned and Stokes said, "Do you mind if I douse the light? Haven't worked so hard since my first week at Annapolis and I'm bone-tired."

Tim was physically tired, but too excited over meeting his old friends and the others to fall asleep. He squirmed and wriggled in his narrow bunk. The whole cruise would be perfect, he thought, if that blamed Stokes hadn't come aboard. Of course, I'm glad he didn't go with the Yanks. One less against us; but why couldn't he have landed on one of those Mississippi gunboats?

Tim twisted over on his other side. Don't know what there is about Stokes, but he always has been able to rile me. Just hope we don't get assigned duties and watches together.

Finally he dozed, but it seemed only minutes before the call to rise and shine sounded.

He groaned, rubbed his eyes sleepily, and got up. He dressed so slowly he was the last one to reach the wardroom.

Tim's fears were confirmed. Stokes and he were assigned to assist the paymaster, Rodell Carney, in counting and listing stores.

Semmes announced that the Portuguese authorities had notified him that he must move from West Angra to East Angra. "It's the official port of entry," he explained to the officers at breakfast. "Since it's a clear day and the water smooth, no reason the work of sorting and counting stores can't go on, while we're underway. We'll go outside the marine league and transship the heavier guns and the remainder of the stores."

"Seeing that you've come so recently from your clerking duties in Richmond," Rodell Carney told Tim as they went on deck, "you may take down our count as Mr. Stokes and I call the inventory. We'll start with the provisions for the galley."

"Aye, aye, sir."

"Just make a rough copy first and this evening you can write the final listings for Captain Semmes and that Scotch fellow who commands the supply ship. You may use my desk for that task." The suave paymaster spoke with the tone of a man conferring a great favor.

Tim nodded, and the dreary task began. There were lists, numbers, boxes, bales, casks. Then the listing of the quantities of pork, beef, butter, salt and sugar. Endlessly it went on. As Stokes and Carney sang out the count, Tim carefully made the four marks and crossed them diagonally with a line, so that the totals could be counted easily in fives.

Tim's lack of sleep was telling. Several times he had to ask for a repeat of the count, until both Carney and Stokes spoke to him sharply, asking him to pay closer attention.

All the time, new stores were being transshipped.

There were noise and confusion, as the big guns were hauled aboard. Tim developed a headache, but he kept at the work doggedly.

It was dusk when the *290* and the supply ship ran into the East Angra Harbor. Tim was at the paymaster's desk, checking and rechecking his counts from the day's inventory and making careful copies in ink for the two ships' commanders.

Tim looked up to rest his eyes and noted through the port that a Portuguese schooner-of-war was anchored near the small fort. They were hailed as they passed, but no one could hear the words.

At last, the copies were finished. Tim left them on the desk and went to his quarters. Too weary to talk, the midshipman dropped off to sleep within minutes of stretching out on his bunk.

Tim had no idea of the time, nor how long he'd slept, when he heard cannons firing. He bolted from his bunk and looked up the hatch, but could see no flash of firing.

Both the fort and the schooner appeared dark, which was puzzling since the sound seemed to have come from the sea. Tim realized how helpless they were since the vessel's batteries were not ready for a fight. Had they been trapped, helpless, by the enemy?

"Maffitt! Anderson! Stokes! Get up! We're being fired on!"

Tim shook the others roughly. The dazed midshipmen were groggy with sleep. Just after Tim roused them, there came the ominous boom of another exploding shell.

In seconds the young officers were dressed and hurtling into the wardroom.

Tim raced to Captain Semmes' cabin, pounded on the door, and shouted, "Firing, sir!"

"How many shots?"

"Three so far, sir."

"Have any of them struck us?"

"No, sir, none. They seem to be firing wild."

"Let him fire away in the dark. I expect he won't hurt us." Captain Semmes opened his door, glanced out and said, "Back to your quarters, gentlemen. You will be called if you are needed."

Tim was sure he couldn't sleep but he obeyed the order. All was quiet now, except for a little grumbling from Stokes.

Next morning Tim was sheepish when he learned the news. A passing mail steamer had run into the anchorage, fired three signal guns for waiting passengers on shore, and departed with them before daylight.

At breakfast, Tim was the target of a lot of jeering comments.

Rodell Carney stroked his waxed mustache tenderly. "I shall rest much better, gentlemen," he said, "now that I am aware we have such an alert young officer aboard. However, it's just possible that it is fortunate for us older, more experienced men that you watchful lads are in the steerage. It would be annoying to be disturbed every night with some minor alarm."

The paymaster's tone was even more sarcastic than his words. Tim flushed but realized that there was no time for resentful thoughts.

The dirty job of coaling was going forward, for the rough passage had used most of the fuel in the cruiser's bunkers. The carpenter and gunner, with the help of the chief engineer, were busy putting down the circles or traverses for the pivot guns. The boatswain and his gang labored at fitting side and train tackles for the broadside battery.

The counting of stores went on. Tim thought wearily that there must be enough stores on board to sustain a crew for years. Six barrels of salt! A whole barrel of pepper. Surely there couldn't be as much shot and shell in the whole world as he had counted. He thought resentfully, after evening mess, as he labored at Carney's desk, that again Stokes had outwitted him. He was at ease, now, while Tim had to go on and on making the final copies of the inventory.

By Saturday night, the coal bunkers were filled, the armament in place, and most of the stores unpacked, counted and distributed.

The tired officers lingered over coffee at dinner. Captain Semmes confessed his chief concern to them. "Tomorrow should settle our most pressing need. We have no enlisted crew. We will have to recruit them from this ship, the *Bahama* and the *Agrippina.*

"In their rags and dirt they aren't a promising lot. With a touch of soap, clean uniforms and a few days of discipline, they will look better." He sighed, then smiled briefly at Tim. "I shall talk to the sailors, after the commissioning ceremony, and then flash the gold. It will be much more effective than my voice, I'm sure."

Tim squared his shoulders in pride and glanced at Rodell Carney, but the paymaster was giving respectful attention to the captain's words. "You gentlemen may be interested in knowing," Semmes continued, "that Mr. Moore made his roundabout way to join us on a mission from Secretary Mallory. He brought a satchel full of gold, which, added to the fifty thousand dollars in sovereigns and the fifty thousand dollars in bank bills I obtained from our agents in England, will tempt a crew tomorrow, I am certain."

Tim thanked the captain with a smile, then looked modestly down at the table. The conversation became general again, and several men asked Tim for news of Richmond and their friends at headquarters.

Enjoying the limelight, the young officer expanded. Desperately he groped for every little bit of gossip and news he could remember. These men, who had been away from their homes for more than a year, listened eagerly as he described the ironclads the Confederates were building at Norfolk and New Orleans. The men lingered, asking more and more questions.

Rodell Carney brought out his big gold watch, then yawned.

"Gentlemen, this has been most enjoyable," Captain Semmes said, "and as much as we like to hear recent news from home, tomorrow we have an important function to perform for our Confederacy. I regret having to end this pleasant evening, but we must be fresh for the ceremony."

Tim lingered contentedly a moment on deck, gazing toward the lights of the shore and humming "Dixie."

"Mr. Moore."

Startled, Tim turned to see the erect figure of Rodell Carney alongside him at the rail.

"Sir?"

"I should like you to recall your Navy training," he said, his voice like ice. "No man, no Virginian in particular, is worthy of being called an officer and a gentleman when he takes over all the conversation at dinner.

"I should like to remind you, Mr. Moore, that your position at Navy headquarters was that of a clerk. One would get the picture from your remarks this evening that at the very least you performed the duties of Under Secretary." He strode away.

For quite a few minutes, Tim clutched the rail, shaking and white with rage and shock, hearing again the cold and sneering voice, the firm and final sounds of Carney's steps on the deck.

Maybe I have been showing off a little, Tim thought resentfully, but no need for him to be so mean and ornery. Why, even Captain Semmes said my talk was enjoyable.

Tim finally went below to his quarters. He was grateful for the dark, and that his mates were already asleep in their bunks.

Why did Carney hate him?

Chapter 4

SIGNING A CREW

SUNDAY dawned a glorious day. Officers and men worked to ready the ship for the important ceremony. Tim, refreshed by sleep and busy at his tasks, put the Carney affair out of his mind. There just wasn't time for bitter thoughts, for anger.

The first lieutenant and officer of the deck took over. In a couple of hours, after hard scrubbing and the use of holystones, the cruiser was neat and clean. The awnings were spread, her yards squared, and with rigging hauled taut, she stood out of the harbor followed by the *Bahama*.

For the first time, the flag of the Confederate States was unfurled. Tim and his fellow officers were in full uniform and even the crew looked more fit.

Captain Semmes summoned all hands to the quarterdeck. There he mounted a gun carriage and read the commission from President Jefferson Davis, appointing him a captain in the Confederate States Navy and the order of Stephen R. Mallory, Secretary of the Navy, directing him to assume command of the *Alabama.*

It was a deeply impressive moment and as Tim stood with bared head, the scene was imprinted in his memory forever.

The formal ceremony ended with the firing of the weather-bow gun and the singing of "Dixie." The *Alabama* was christened.

Captain Semmes then addressed the sailors. "You may have passage back to England on the *Bahama* and your pay will continue until Liverpool." He paused. "It is your free choice.

"The Southern States in our Confederacy," he went on, his black eyes flashing with feeling and his voice deep with emotion, "being sovereign and independent, have dissolved the league that held us with the Northern States. We are now threatened with subjugation by our former countrymen."

Again he paused. Tim glanced at the unpromising lot of sailors, unmoved by this plea. They were English, Dutch, Spanish, Italian, French, Irish. Obviously, they weren't concerned with the rights and wrongs of this struggle.

Captain Semmes shrewdly and cleverly shifted his argument. "You men have sailed this fine new ship and know well how sturdily she weathers a gale. I don't have to point out her merits to you. We propose a cruise now to all the major seas and ports of the world. You went to sea because you wanted to see faraway places. That we can promise!"

He signalled to Lieutenant Kell, who produced the satchel of gold with a flourish. The bright gold pieces sparkled in the sunshine. The captain's eyes glinted as he added, "You will receive double the ordinary wages."

Word was passed around the crewmen that those who wished to stay with the *Alabama* were to see the paymaster and sign the articles.

Eighty of the ninety men available from the crews of the *290* and the *Bahama* signed. They drove hard bargains. Stokers got 7 pounds per month; ordinary seamen 4 pounds, 10 shillings. With no living expenses, these were generous wages.

It was a busy day for Captain Semmes. Assisted by Captain Bulloch, Captain Butcher, the paymaster and the clerk, he made out the half-pay tickets. These were advances on wages to be delivered to sweethearts, mothers or wives at home.

It was 11 o'clock that night before all the paper work was finished.

Captain Butcher was to return to England with Captain Bulloch. After farewells, they sailed away on the *Bahama*.

The supply ship departed with a skeleton crew. Many of her men had signed on the cruiser.

Tim, weary to the point of complete exhaustion, turned away to go to his bunk. Unexpectedly, he faced Rodell Carney, who said sternly, "Come with me to Captain Semmes' cabin."

Tim, though very puzzled, followed him.

Stokes was standing at ease in front of Captain Semmes' desk. That officer, stony-faced, was looking at the inventories Tim had written and was checking them with another list.

"Mr. Moore, there seems to be a serious discrepancy in several categories of your listing of stores. It's too late now for a re-count, since we've paid the Scotch captain and he has sailed."

Tim stared at Captain Semmes, unable to believe this nightmare was really happening.

The captain went on. "You've put down 30 barrels of pork, when we have only 20. You've listed 40 barrels of powder and we have 25." He looked again at the lists. "Those are apparently only a few of the errors. Here's an item of 6 barrels of salt and it should be 4. Mr. Carney did a quick re-count this afternoon, but didn't have an opportunity to check your inventories until the last hour. Have you an explanation?"

Tim, flushing miserably, found he couldn't talk. Finally he managed, "I—I can't understand it, sir. I checked and rechecked my first lists." He turned to Rodell Carney. "Sir, do you still have my first counts? If we could check them—"

"No, of course not," the older man said sharply. "I try to keep my desk shipshape, and I'm not in the habit of hanging on to obsolete materials. When you turned over the final copies, I destroyed the original count sheets."

Helplessly, Tim turned back to the captain. "May I see them, please?"

There was no doubt that it was his own handwriting. "I can't explain it, sir," he said with as much dignity as he could manage.

Stokes coughed softly and said, "If you please, Captain Semmes. Mr. Moore was apparently very tired after his rough trip out here. He asked us to repeat the count to him time after time. It must just be an honest mistake." He sounded genuine and sincere.

Captain Semmes was grim. "No question of Mr. Moore's honesty is implied. I am sure Secretary Mallory would not have given him the responsibility of delivering that sum of gold unless he was sure of Mr. Moore's integrity.

"It is too late now to rectify the costly error, but from now on I believe it would be better not to use Mr. Moore's services to our cause in counting and listing stores."

He thrust the inventories and the other lists into a drawer of his desk. "Right now, we must get on with our tasks. The executive officer wants all hands on deck. Will you report there immediately?"

Rodell Carney and Clint Stokes exchanged an odd look, which Tim, in his misery, failed to see.

When they reached the deck, Lieutenant Kell was speaking. "Since it will take all day tomorrow, at least, to set up regular assignments for watches and stations, I'd like to call for volunteers for tonight's watches."

Every man stepped forward promptly and Kell smiled. "That's the right spirit," he said, "but it looks as if I'll have to set up the temporary watches by lot."

"If I may, Lieutenant Kell, make a suggestion?" It was Rodell Carney's smooth voice.

"Certainly, sir."

"I should like to ask the favor of having Midshipman Stokes and myself excused from watches. We have an almost overwhelming task in completing the checking and listing of stores, supplies, ammunition and the like, which will take us from dawn to dusk. Since Mr. Stokes was my assistant on the *Sumter* and we're used to working together, I should like to bid for his assistance on this new cruise."

Kell nodded in agreement.

The *Alabama* sailed serenely northeast, with fore-and-aft sails set. Tim had drawn the midnight watch and his mind went back, again and again, to the enmity of the paymaster.

Miserably, he recalled the recent scene in the captain's cabin. How could he have made so many mistakes? Couldn't Stokes and Carney have been wrong in their counting?

As he paced and thought during the lonely darkness, Tim suddenly straightened to his full height. After all the months of waiting, I am at last on a Confederate ship-of-war, he told himself proudly. It's what I've wanted ever since secession. I know I've made a real contribution to our cause by bringing that gold to Captain Semmes. No one can take that away from me.

Chapter 5

FIRST CAPTURES

TIM was making his bunk when he heard his name called. He snapped to attention when he saw Lieutenant Kell outside in the passageway. "Yes, sir!"

The older officer was holding a thick sheaf of papers in his hand. "I understand you've been doing a lot of clerking?"

Tim swallowed painfully and blushed. "Yes, sir. I reckon I didn't do such a good job listing stores. Captain Semmes doesn't think I should do that any more."

"I know about that, but this duty will be slightly different. Come along to my cabin after mess and we'll get started."

Tim smiled broadly, and there was relief in his voice as he answered, "I'll do my best, sir. Thank you."

"I know you understand we can't overlook another mistake."

"Yes, sir." Tim's hands trembled as he folded his blankets. His mind went back again and again to the inventory. Couldn't Carney and Stokes have made the errors in counting? He *knew* their count had been 6 barrels of salt and not 4, because he'd asked to have it repeated twice. He shook his head. He couldn't waste any more time puzzling over that dratted inventory.

Tim hoped that this temporary clerking assignment would lead to his being one of Kell's permanent assistants. He'd learned to admire the older man's sturdy character, courage and evident loyalty to the Confederacy.

One of Tim's first duties was to help draw up the station-bill. This was the assignment for each officer and man on board in battle, on watch, or in pursuit of enemy ships.

At mess Tim confided to Eugene Maffitt, "I've been glad for the last few weeks of being at sea before actually reporting for duty. A year of clerking made me forget my seamanship. Today, I've been glad I had all that time clerking. Jiminy! I never had to write so many names and numbers so fast."

Maffitt grinned. "I'm plumb crazy trying to remember my own positions. Been going around muttering to myself, 'Starboard watch; third division of the battery; gun 3!' Why don't you and Lieutenant Kell figure out a little verse for each of us to learn? It would be a lot easier."

"It's all we can do to get out the station-bill," Tim retorted. "If you forget, you can always take a look at it. I have a feeling, though, that we'll be so well drilled in another 3 days we won't have a chance to forget."

Below decks a great deal of hard work remained. However, after the men had been assigned to berths and messes and all had memorized their stations and quarters, the cruiser swiftly assumed the neat look of a man-of-war.

"I thought we might be making a capture right away, sir," Tim remarked to Lieutenant Kell, when that busy man paused for coffee.

"It won't be long, Mr. Moore. You'll find Captain Semmes is remarkably efficient. He has withdrawn from the trade routes for a few days. You'll note the steam is down, the screw hoisted, and we are under easy sail. That is to allow us to get the crew and officers familiar with all their duties. We will have gun drill several times in the next few days. Several of the crew have served on ships-of-war and will make good drill sergeants for the others."

"I heard a rumor that we're going for the whaling fleet."

"It's the height of the season and the whale fisheries are close. The season won't last more than another 6 weeks." He fingered his bushy brown beard thoughtfully, then sighed. "We must get on with our work, Mr. Moore."

The first capture, a few days later, was surprisingly easy.

The lookout sighted a whaler, lying to, with her fore-topsail to the mast.

Hoisting the Union colors as a disguise, the cruiser made sail for her. When within boarding distance of a few hundred yards, the Confederate banner replaced the enemy flag.

The surprise was complete and it was not even necessary to fire a gun.

The *Ocmulgee* of Edgartown, Massachusetts, had just struck a huge whale, which was partially hoisted out of the water by her yard tackles. The Yankee skipper and his crew of thirty-six men were taken on board the raider. The boats were busy, plying back and forth, removing small stores, beef and pork from the whaler.

It was 9 p.m. when the last of the boats pulled away from the capture, but Captain Semmes waited until daylight to burn it. A fire at night would have been a warning to other whalers in the vicinity.

It was a beautiful setting for the *Alabama*'s first muster, the following day. Captain Semmes liked to have this ceremony of dress and inspection on Sunday.

Tim felt immense pride in his ship as he stood at attention, listening to the captain read the Articles of War. Her sails were neatly trimmed, the decks clean and white and the brasswork glittered like mirrors in the sun.

When the muster was completed, Tim and the other midshipmen leaned on the rail to watch the prisoners from the capture leave the ship in their own whaleboats, which had been towed along.

"They're really loaded to the top," Tim remarked idly.

Maffitt nodded. "Captain Semmes allowed them to take their personal possessions and plenty of provisions. Look's as if they took him at his word."

"They'll have enough food to feed the United States consul and family, when they reach that island," Stokes added. "Of course, it may be a week or so before they'll be picked up and returned North."

Tim turned from the rail and surveyed the shining

decks again, smiling. "She looks quite different from two weeks ago."

Maffitt tugged at his jacket. "So do the rest of us. Never would have believed the crew could look so good."

"Clean ducks and polished shoes help," Anderson contributed, "but washing off the coal dust made the biggest change."

Tim agreed. "I didn't even recognize Sam Storr for a minute or so, when I saw him with his hair and beard combed and cut."

While they still stood at ease along the rail, the cry of "Sail ho!" rang out. Immediately, the raider put about and sailed toward the approaching schooner.

Captain Semmes' order came swiftly. "Bend on and hoist a British flag!" This ruse was intended to throw the stranger off guard.

Tim took his station alongside Lieutenant Kell, ready to race with new orders. Both ships were under fast sail and in less than an hour were a mile apart.

"She's shown no colors, sir," Tim said.

Kell nodded grimly. "She's got every stitch of canvas set and she's edging off a little."

Tim was anxious. "Soon she'll be sheltered in the marine league. Neutral land is only about 5 miles away."

"Exactly."

At that moment Captain Semmes gave the order

to Lieutenant Kell to fire a blank cartridge and heave the schooner to.

The schooner preferred the race. Tim pounded the rail in his excitement. This was more like it! The first capture of the whaler had been tame.

The *Alabama,* smartly handled, was gaining rapidly. A round shot from the bow gun spoke with authority.

Breathlessly, the officers and crew of the raider stared across the water. Seconds later the graceful little craft luffed up in the wind, brailing up her foresail and hauling her jib sheet to windward.

The capture was the schooner *Starlight* of Boston.

At mess that night Captain Semmes told his officers, "We captured newspapers and papers on board the enemy. The United States consul at Fayal reported, in his dispatches to Secretary Seward in Washington, that 'rebel privateers' and 'pirates' are operating in these waters."

He smiled grimly, but his black eyes were flashing. "We will be called many harsh and insulting names by our enemies. I want all of you to remember and be proud of the fact that you are Southern officers and gentlemen, fighting for our Confederate States, in a commissioned man-of-war. The stratagem of using British and other flags as a disguise is just that, a justifiable piece of war trickery. Our job is to attack and destroy enemy merchant shipping. The more successful we are, the harder words will be hurled at us."

Next morning, the passengers from the *Starlight* and the paroled prisoners from her crew were landed at Santa Cruz.

That afternoon the cruiser overtook a large ship, the *Ocean Rover* of New Bedford, Massachusetts. She had been out more than 3 years and had sent home two cargoes of oil. At their own request, the Yankees were allowed to row in their whaleboats to land, 5 miles away.

Then the *Alabama* had its first all-night chase.

Tim's watch ended at 4 a.m., but the pursuit of the speedy sailing ship flitting just ahead in the moonlight was too exciting to miss.

Finally captured, the *Alert,* just out of New London and bound for the Indian Ocean with stores of clothing, choice beef, pork, soap and tobacco, proved a rich prize. Again, officers and crew were paroled and sent ashore in their own boats.

Captain Semmes then gave the order to fire all three captures.

"Mr. Moore. You'll come with me." It was Arthur Sinclair giving the order, since he was in command of the second quarterboat.

"Aye, aye, sir!" Tim scrambled down the ladder eagerly. It was the first time he'd been ordered out, and with a high sense of adventure he found a place in the bobbing boat, next to Sam Storr.

The old salt was calmly chewing his cud of tobacco, his hands on an oar.

"This is what I've been wanting to do," Tim said, with satisfaction. "I didn't come to sea just to do more clerking."

The grizzled old sailor gave the young man a sardonic look but said nothing.

Never had Tim had his mind changed so quickly. This duty was the most unpleasant he'd ever faced.

The *Alert,* so trim and swift and graceful in last night's chase was a chaotic shamble. The deck was strewn with broken cases and discarded articles in an unsightly jumble. Two sailors raced for the forecastle, carrying their dark lanterns, and the coxswain ran to the main hold.

Lieutenant Sinclair signalled to Tim to follow. They entered the captain's cabin. Charts, papers, books had been ruthlessly torn and tossed on the floor. "Gather up an armload of these. Toss 'em on the captain's bunk and pour that can of whale oil over the mess."

Tim, jaw set grimly, obeyed the order. He hadn't fully realized until this moment the wicked waste of war.

It had been spectacular, almost like fireworks, to see the blaze of the burning *Ocmulgee* across the water. Starting the fire with the candle from one's own lantern was different, and ugly.

Sinclair worked swiftly, gathering more papers,

tearing leaves from books to throw in the flames. "That'll do it," he said. "Pour on all the oil—"

The deck rocked under them from a terrific explosion, and the two turned to race from the cabin.

The flames were crackling just a few feet away and the whole ship shook violently again from two more explosions. "We'll have to dive overboard," Sinclair shouted, running. "We can't get to the ladder."

Tim and he dove overboard. It was terrifying to feel the searing heat and breathe the acrid smoke. The plunge from blinding light to dark waters seemed to take a long time.

Fortunately, a number of cases and spars had been thrown overboard earlier and several sailors, many of whom were poor swimmers, had managed to save themselves by clinging to the floating wood.

Tim, who had always been a strong swimmer, helped several men into the quarterboat. Sinclair, too, was skillful in the water and he circled the boat for a last look before climbing over the side. The glare from the blazing ship lighted the scene. Sinclair counted. "All here!" he sang out in relief.

"I won't do that no more," Sam Storr declared, trying to wring out his sodden jacket.

"What did happen?" Tim asked. "All we heard was the explosion and the whole ship shook under us."

"I busted open some barrels of turpentine in the hold and threw torches across at 'em. Never been so dry and hot and so wet and cold so fast, ever, and I ain't aimin' to try it again."

Before the quarterboat reached the *Alabama,* great shoots of fire burst from the other ships, outlining the drooping, dead canvas.

Tim, pulling on his oar, thought the sound of the crisp crackle and hissing of the blazes, the sight of the three doomed ships sinking in the black waters, would haunt his dreams forever.

Chapter 6

MYSTERY ON SHORE

IN mid-October, the raider cruised closer to the Banks of Newfoundland. Now Tim learned the bitter truth that the most treacherous enemy of all at sea could be violent weather. The water and wind had a malice that seemed to have a personal spite. He was always tired, always wet, always hungry. It was an effort to sleep, wedged in his bunk against the vicious rolling of the ship.

Everyone was equally miserable and cheerless. As the midshipmen lay awake after their watches one night, Maffitt complained, "Thought I could live my whole life happily without another bowl of beans. Right now, I'd give my next 6 months' pay for just one, if it were good and hot."

"Coffee. I keep trying to remember what it smells like and how it tastes," Anderson added. "The galley's been awash for days."

"I'd make my deal for some dry clothes. I'm sure

my uniforms are more wet salt than wool." Tim wriggled restlessly in his bunk.

Stokes jeered at Tim. "Wish you were warm and dry and safe back in Richmond? After all, the rest of us have had a year more of this gay life on the bounding main than you."

Tim couldn't sleep. It wasn't just physical discomfort that kept him awake. So, now I've got two enemies aboard, he told himself. Carney and Stokes never miss a chance to throw a spike at me. Stokes and I weren't really friendly at Annapolis, but it wasn't until I blurted out I thought he'd gone with the Yankees that he took this open dislike to me. If only I'd learn to hold my tongue.

Still the grim chase went on. There were so many captures, Tim lost track of the names.

One of the ships yielded a prize of six live pigs, which furnished a welcome addition of fresh pork to the diet. At sea more than 70 days, many of the men on board the raider were showing definite symptoms of scurvy.

At the end of October, only 200 miles from New York, both officers and men were bone-weary of fighting storms and the punishing labor of making captures in rough seas.

Captain Semmes called a meeting of the officers in the wardroom. "We have only 4 days' supply of coal left," he announced, "so we're going to rendezvous with our supply ship in the West Indies." The news was greeted with cheers.

It was pleasant sailing into warmer waters and Tim looked forward eagerly to going ashore in the French port of Fort de France on the Island of Martinique. He was delighted to be ordered to the boat which was landing prisoners.

The *Agrippina,* loaded with coal for the raider's bunkers, was at anchor nearby.

Tim donned his best gold and gray uniform and waited for the signal to leave. Unexpectedly, he was summoned to Captain Semmes' cabin. "Mr. Moore, I should like you to do an errand for me. Please mail these letters and go to the stationer's for envelopes and writing paper. If you are able to find any recent newspapers from New York or Boston, I should be obliged."

He gave Tim some coins and the young officer saluted smartly. "Aye, aye, sir. Is there anything else?"

"No. The boat will return 1 hour after docking."

"Yes, sir."

Tim had hoped to have time for a meal ashore, but even an hour in this picturesque little port, in the bright sunshine, made his spirits soar. Besides, the galley would have fresh fruits and vegetables from the markets.

He chuckled at the odd feeling it gave him to walk on solid land. It had been so many months!

Tim's French was faulty, but by pointing at envelopes and letter pads, he was able to make his wants known. The only newspapers for sale were French, so Tim decided to use his precious hour by looking for the Northern newspapers elsewhere. It was a treat to stroll the narrow sidewalks, eying the brightly clad natives and listening to the foreign speech.

Down one narrow side street, Tim was startled to see Rodell Carney, arm in arm with the gray-haired Scotch captain of the *Agrippina.*

How had Carney come ashore? He must have arrived with the men sent to market.

As Tim was puzzled, he followed them down the little street. The paymaster and the Scotsman were

entering a small saloon. Their manner was almost furtive.

Tim, resentful of Carney's superior airs from the beginning of the cruise, was curious. Boldly he followed the pair into the dark little restaurant. He was just in time to see them disappearing into a room above, which opened on a shadowy balcony. The door closed firmly behind them.

A fierce-looking man with sharp eyes and bristling mustache addressed Tim in a rush of French from behind the bar. Tim, noting the man's filthy apron and the array of bottles back of him, muttered, "No, thank you, I was just looking for a friend," and backed out.

The sunny street looked warm and friendly. As Tim strolled back to the main street, he thought how odd the incident had been. He had seen the dour and silent old captain of the *Agrippina* several times at Terceira, before the arrival of the other Confederate officers. The Scotch captain had remained aloof from the English officers on board the ship.

Carney must have known him previously, since they were so friendly now. However, Tim could not recall the paymaster's having mentioned it. Then he shrugged; after all, he had an errand to do for Captain Semmes.

Tim was unable to find any recent British or Union newspapers. Back on shipboard, Tim went in search of the captain. When he couldn't find him, he left the packages and unspent coins on the table.

The captain and the paymaster were both absent from noon mess.

Later that afternoon, Tim was puzzled to see the supply ship setting sail out of the harbor.

There was an atmosphere of ugliness and suspicion all over the ship. Sailors and officers alike were disgruntled at having no liberty ashore.

Captain Semmes that evening in the wardroom was openly annoyed. He made no secret of the cause of his anger. "Gentlemen, you have wondered why no shore leaves have been granted, and why the *Agrippina* left the harbor this afternoon.

"I regret to inform you that the captain of the supply ship has been here 8 days, and has been most indiscreet. On shore he announced to all and sundry that he was to meet the *Alabama*. There has been more than sufficient time for word to get to our enemy.

"I had no choice but to set another secret rendezvous. I should have liked to have sailed at once, but it is necessary for us to take on food supplies. We shall leave at the earliest possible moment, although it may still be too late."

"Why, I saw the old Scotch captain and Mr. Carney this morning!" Tim exclaimed, almost without thinking. "They were going into a saloon down a side street, jabbering away like old friends. I thought it was strange, because the old fellow was anything but friendly when we were loading at Terceira."

Rodell Carney leaped to his feet, his eyes blazing. "Mr. Moore! Do you mean to insinuate that I am a traitor to our glorious cause? Why, you young, conceited, stupid—"

"That will be enough!" Captain Semmes roared. "Mr. Moore, you will apologize at once."

Tim, his voice shaky, said, "Why, I didn't mean anything like that. I didn't realize how it would sound. I only thought it was odd to see them together."

"Please sit down and finish your meal, Mr. Carney. It was unfortunate that the captain talked too freely, but I intended no suggestion of disloyalty. You will forget this exchange, gentlemen."

Tim was pointedly left out of the conversation for the rest of the meal. He was bewildered and hurt at the attitude of his fellow officers.

There had been something secret and furtive in that meeting he had chanced to see on shore that morning. He realized, however, that it had been a mistake to blurt out his suspicions in front of all the officers.

The next morning Captain Semmes' fears were realized. Just outside the marine league at the mouth of the harbor, the formidable Union ship-of-war, *San Jacinto,* was idly cruising.

The men on the *Alabama* didn't have to use glasses to see the enemy's decks were cleared for action.

The Union ship had guns run out and ready.

Chapter 7

YANKEE SKIPPER

NEUTRALITY rules were clear and understood by all. If ships owned by enemies entered a neutral harbor, such as Fort de France, one must remain for 24 hours after the other sailed.

Therefore, the Union battleship carefully kept outside the marine league. The *San Jacinto* would pounce on the Confederate raider the moment she left the shelter of the French harbor and was outside the safe zone. The men on the raider were tense, silent, knowing the dangers of the ordeal ahead.

In the late afternoon, Tim was among the first to glimpse the huge black rain squall rolling up from starboard.

"Never thought I'd be so glad to see a storm blowing up," he said to Anderson. "We might have a chance—"

"If it just keeps on coming!"

With night, the torrents fell and every man on deck was immediately drenched. They waited hours in the darkness, trying to see through the downpour. Not a light was permitted.

At midnight the crew was ordered to quarters. Guns were loaded and run out. With a full head of steam, the sleek vessel slipped from port, running to the south.

Tim, unmindful now of his soaked clothing, stood alertly at his station. All was unnaturally still on board and Tim scarcely dared to breathe. Orders were whispered. He lost all track of time and the night seemed endless. Each minute of the suspense seemed to last a month. It was hard to believe it was only 1 o'clock when Lieutenant Kell, speaking in normal tones, passed along the word from Captain Semmes to relieve all hands, except the starboard watch, and to run in the guns.

The *Alabama* had escaped the enemy!

The new rendezvous was reached the following afternoon. The *Agrippina* and the cruiser ran into the anchorage together at Blanquilla, a little barren island, off the coast of Venezuela.

The men on the raider were startled to find a Yankee whaling schooner at this remote and lonely spot. Her crew had pitched a tent on the beach and had some boilers going, trying out the oil from a whale.

The *Alabama* was flying the Union flag.

The schooner sent off a boat to meet the raider, bringing the Yankee captain.

Captain Semmes greeted him as he climbed the ladder. "I've come to pilot y' in safely," the visitor announced. "And it's good y've come. That dratted *Alabama* has been playin' hob with our fleet."

"That so?" Captain Semmes inquired. "Fast sail, is she?"

"Turrible. Turrible. Catches everything afore her." He gazed about him. "Looks like you got a very trim ship here, though. Never see such a sight o' guns. 'Pears to me you got just the vessel to give that pirate, Semmes, what he's got comin'."

Tim, standing nearby with Anderson and Maffitt, didn't dare look at either. This was really comical! Anderson's tall shoulders were heaving as he tried to choke back his laughter; Maffitt managed to change his chuckles into a coughing spell.

"Come on," Tim muttered, leading the way to the other side of the deck. "We can't give the show away."

Several other officers had found the scene too much for them and were huddled, laughing, out of hearing and sight of the two captains.

The Yankee spent a happy half hour, until the anchor was dropped. Then Captain Semmes, still with a straight face, informed him he was on board the *Alabama*.

The old captain was speechless, dismay on his rugged features. After a long and embarrassing silence, Captain Semmes went on in his most gentle voice. "You have nothing to fear, skipper. You are safe here. Out of respect for Venezuela's jurisdiction, where we both are, we shall not burn your boat or your oil. I shall ask you to give me your word, sir, not to depart ahead of us. I do not wish you to carry word to our enemy."

"Yes. Oh, yes, sir!"

Captain Semmes paused and then his voice deepened. "Of course, if you do sail at night, we should have to overtake you and burn your ship, because then you would no longer be protected by the neutrality laws."

For 5 days, the coaling operations continued. There was hard work for everyone. The hold was broken out for the first time, scrubbed and freshly whitewashed.

For most of the men, it was the first time to leave the ship in more than 3 months. The crew was allowed to go on shore in quarter watches to enjoy fishing, swimming and hunting.

This pleasant interlude was soon over, however, and a few days later Tim went along with a boarding party to a schooner stopped by the raider. She proved to be Spanish, recently from Boston, and the captain obligingly gave an armful of recent newspapers from the city to Lieutenant Sinclair.

As they rowed back to the cruiser, the officer read

headlines and bits of news to the men. They all had a good laugh when he read, " 'There are no Union cruisers in the gulf and the Confederate raider, *Alabama,* is on her way to the coast of Brazil and the West Indies.' "

Sinclair opened another paper and whistled. "General Banks is fitting out an expedition in Boston with an army of thirty thousand Yankees. They're to sail in transports to Galveston, Texas, which was recently captured by Union forces. They aim to take the whole state."

The news of the fall of Galveston was a blow, but Tim wasn't the only one to catch the connection between the two pieces of news. Unarmed transports with no Union cruisers to convoy them through the gulf! These could be rich prizes for the Confederate raider.

Then, in a happy mood, Lieutenant Sinclair read the timetables of arrivals and departures of California steamers to and from New York. It wouldn't be such bad luck to capture one of those gold-laden vessels.

Back on board the raider, Tim reported the important news gleaned from the Yankee newspapers to Lieutenant Kell. "If we could catch those army transports with no Yankee men-of-war about, what a blow we could strike."

The older man stroked his brown beard thoughtfully, but he was smiling at Tim's eagerness. "It would be quite a fish fry. Remember, though, that first, we must catch our fish."

A few nights later at evening mess, Captain Semmes took the officers into his confidence. "The Banks expedition from Boston cannot reach Galveston much before mid-January, 6 weeks from now. We'll ply the east end of Cuba, under easy sail, for a time. It's a much-traveled waterway and we should have easy hunting."

Word spread over the raider that a large freighter, carrying gold, was due from California.

The regular watches promptly volunteered for overtime work, to catch her.

"Sail ho!" startled the officers from their breakfast.

"Where away?" came immediately from the trumpet of the officer of the deck.

"Broad on the port bow, sir!"

"Can you make her out?"

By this time, every officer and man had swarmed to the deck.

"She is a large steamer, brig-rigged, sir!"

"All hands work ship!" The engineers and firemen worked with a will.

Tim took his station by the side of Lieutenant Kell. He saw that the stranger was a packet ship, also under steam.

It was a colorful sight. The sky was bright and the balmiest of breezes was blowing. In the distance, the islands of Cuba, Santo Domingo and Jamaica could be seen in vivid blues and greens. The packet had her awnings set, and in the shade were men, mostly in uniform, women in gay bonnets and frocks, and several active children.

The raider veered and unfurled the Confederate flag. It was close enough to detect the alarm on the big passenger ship. The women screamed and scampered below decks, herding all of the children before them.

The captain of the packet decided to make a run

for it. It was instantly clear that the packet had more speed than the *Alabama.*

Captain Semmes ordered the rifled bow gun to be cleared away.

The gun crew was told to take aim at the packet's foremast, high enough above deck not to endanger lives. The gun spoke and splinters high on the mast proved the accuracy of the range.

The great wheels of the steamer slowed to a stop.

The capture of the *Ariel* replaced muster that Sunday morning, December 7, 1862.

The prize was a California steamer, true, but instead of being homeward bound with a million dollars in gold, she was outward bound with five hundred passengers on board. There were also one hundred officers and soldiers, all of whom were deprived of their arms and paroled.

The boarding officer returned with the news that the women were in tears and hysterics.

Captain Semmes, smiling, summoned Lieutenant Armstrong. He ordered him to array himself in his newest gray and gold uniform, buckle on the best sword in the wardroom, the brightest sword-knot, and return for orders.

"You are to go on board the *Ariel* and coax the ladies out of their hysterics," the captain said when Armstrong returned. "You may go in my gig."

"Aye, aye, sir. I'll be sure to carry out those orders." He grinned. "I never knew a fair creature who could resist me more than 15 minutes."

The other officers hooted and jeered. They laughed even harder when the handsome lieutenant returned an hour later, bedraggled and buttonless, but smiling in triumph.

"They were weeping and wailing," he reported to Captain Semmes, "when I asked to be shown to the ladies' cabins. Even I was taken aback, but only for a moment. I said to them, 'Ladies! The captain of the *Alabama* has heard of your distress and has sent me on board to calm your fears. I assure you that you have fallen into the hands of Southern gentlemen, under whose protection you are entirely safe. We are by no means the ruffians and outlaws we have been pictured by your people, and you have nothing whatever to fear.' "

Lieutenant Kell, his eyes twinkling, asked, "Then, I take it, they literally tore you apart?"

The young officer blushed, but he was still smiling. "Well, they stopped crying and I walked among them, turning a few compliments. One of the young beauties finally asked if she might not have one of my buttons, as a souvenir of her adventure with the *Alabama.*" He shrugged. "I couldn't refuse, since my orders had been to coax the ladies out of their hysterics. I couldn't run the risk of sending them all back into the vapors. So, when another young lady approached, scissors in hand, what could I do?"

Tim, glancing at his own uniform buttons, thought the young women had acquired choice souvenirs. He'd always admired the button design of a full-rigged ship at sea, circled by eleven stars within a circle of rope.

Captain Semmes kept a prize crew aboard the capture, hoping to seize another merchant ship on which he could place the prisoners and passengers.

Captain Cornelius Vanderbilt of New York, owner of the *Ariel,* was a bitter enemy of the Confederacy. The raider's officers would have taken great satisfaction in destroying his packet.

After several days of sailing alongside the capture, Rodell Carney spoke up at evening mess. "Sir," he addressed Captain Semmes, "it appears we aren't likely to seize another enemy ship soon, so we can transfer our—our guests. It's been almost a week since we've sighted a sail other than the *Ariel.*"

"I am aware of that unfortunate fact, Mr. Carney. Do you have a suggestion?"

The paymaster went on smoothly. "Only that we must prepare for bigger game. Much satisfaction as it would give each one of us to destroy Captain Vanderbilt's valuable ship, I feel we may be wasting time in this escort endeavor." Then he chuckled. "We still may find a packet coming *from* California, on our way to more important prey."

Captain Semmes sighed. "I fear you may be right, sir. We'll delay one more day, then put the prize on ransom bond and release her."

Double watches were assigned, but still no enemy shipping was sighted. Reluctantly, Captain Semmes carried out his own word.

A day or so later, one of the valve castings on the engine of the raider needed repairs, so she was anchored out of the lane of ship traffic on the north side of Jamaica. The chief engineer and his assistants took over for 2 days. The rasp of files, the hammering on the anvil and the blowing bellows sounded constantly.

Tim was puzzled because they sighted no sails. After the daily gun drill, he turned to Lieutenant

Kell and said, "Sir, why haven't we seen any shipping for more than 2 weeks?"

"Captain Semmes' hope and plan is that no other sails shall sight us," he replied. "He wishes to have our whereabouts unreported to the enemy until we have our chance to strike at the Banks expedition."

"Jiminy! That's what I hoped you'd say, sir!"

Chapter 8

ENEMY WARSHIP

IT was an odd holiday week. Christmas was observed only by a solemn religious service in the morning. Captain Semmes wisely kept the officers and crew busy. There just wasn't time to be homesick.

At last, 5 days after the New Year, the commander announced the ship was ready. They set out under sail for Galveston.

The lookouts were posted and warned to keep a weather eye open for a great fleet outside a lighthouse. During the late afternoon of January 11, 1863, the cry came. "Land ho! Sail ho!"

But only five steamers could be seen, and they looked like ships-of-war, not transports.

While this unexpected news was spreading over the ship, a shell could be seen bursting over the city.

"We have recaptured Galveston!" Captain Semmes cried delightedly. "Union warships wouldn't be shelling their own people."

The recapture of Galveston by Confederate forces would explain the absence of the Banks expedition's transports. Without this important harbor, there would be no base from which the Union general could attempt his plan to capture all of Texas.

While the men were still considering this surprising turn, the lookout shouted, "One of the ships is coming out, sir! She's going to chase us!"

Captain Semmes quickly gave his orders to Lieutenant Kell. Sails were unfurled and propeller lowered, but speed kept down as the raider stood away. As night fell, the distance between the two ships was still too great to be sure of the Union ship's build and rig.

When the *Alabama* had decoyed the pursuer 20 miles from the rest of the fleet, the order came to furl sails, beat to quarters and clear for action.

The raider turned to meet her foe. When the enemies were only 100 yards apart, both stopped their engines. "What ship is that?" came the hail from the pursuer.

"This is Her Britannic Majesty's Steamer *Petrel,*" Lieutenant Kell replied, shouting through his leather speaking trumpet.

There was a pause, then Lieutenant Kell hailed in turn.

The reply was indistinct, but most of the men on board the cruiser could hear, "This is the United States——"

Again a silence, then the Yankee voice shouted, "If you please, I will send a boat to board you."

The men on the raider were tensely waiting the next move. Captain Semmes' voice came, cool and reassuring. "Lieutenant Kell, are you ready for action?"

"We are only waiting your word."

"Then tell the enemy who we are. When you have done so, give him a broadside."

Tim, next to the lieutenant, thrilled as he heard Kell shout triumphantly, "This is the Confederate States Steamer *Alabama!*"

The crews were at their gun stations, sights on the enemy and lockstrings in hand.

"Fire!"

There was no moon, but the night was clear. Vis-

ibility was fair. Kell issued his messages to Tim with great rapidity, as he noted the effect of the fire.

Long ago at the Naval Academy, during sleepless nights, Tim had worried about his reaction to facing fire. There had been some harrowing tales about trained Navy men who had turned cowardly in actual battle.

The raider shuddered as a shell struck a few feet from Tim, splintered the deck, but failed to explode.

Two more shots struck the main rigging and dropped into the coal bunkers. Stupidly, Tim stared at the destruction; suddenly the noise seemed dim, far away. He must not lose his head!

Lieutenant Kell shouted an order at Tim.

"What? I can't hear!"

"Tell gun 5 to–boom!–range. Change elevation to–boom! boom!–charge by 2 pounds!"

Tim nodded and raced desperately to carry the orders to gun 5 crew on the deck below.

Unfortunately, he had misunderstood the command and hadn't dared delay to ask to have it repeated a third time. The explosions from his own ship's guns had been so loud he hadn't heard the important order to *decrease* the charge by 2 pounds. He assumed the lieutenant's command had been to increase.

For the rest of the brief engagement, the fire from gun 5 was useless, hurtling over and beyond the target.

Only 13 minutes from the first round of shooting, the Union warship hoisted a light and fired an off-gun as a signal of defeat.

Captain Semmes ordered a cease fire. The *Alabama* steamed closer and received the formal surrender from the enemy captain, who also asked for all boats. His ship was sinking rapidly.

The boats were lowered, and Tim worked with a will in the dark waters, diving overboard three times to pull floundering sailors to safety.

Tim had recovered from his first panic, and was aware, now that the worst of the noise and smoke were gone, that his ship's wounds were not serious. One boat had been demolished but no shots had hit below the water line.

The *Hatteras,* for that was the name of the Union warship, went down quickly. She had managed to lower her own boats in time. With the aid of the rescuers from the raider, all hands, 108 men, were saved.

The prisoners, most of them soaking wet, were gathered on the top deck. After a few minutes, Captain Semmes ordered all the lights put out.

It was full speed ahead for the passage to Yucatan. The furious sounds of battle would have carried to the enemy fleet. The chase would be on at once.

Tim made his way to the wardroom for coffee and hot food. He was wet and exhausted. A half-dozen officers had the same idea, but Tim was the only one in sodden clothing. Rodell Carney, his uniform fresh and hair unruffled, eyed Tim coldly.

"You were of great assistance to the enemy tonight. I understand you are responsible for the miserable performance of gun 5."

Tim, shocked at the attack, looked around the wardroom in dismay. No one seemed smiling and triumphant after the victory.

Clint Stokes put down his coffee cup. "You've been busy, as anyone can see, rescuing your Yankee friends from their salty baths."

Chapter 9

SHARKS AND THE PAYMASTER

TIM was miserable. It had been a mistake not to get Lieutenant Kell's command correctly. A serious mistake, but an understandable one, in the excitement and noise of his first real battle.

It was only Christian duty to rescue any human in danger, even a hated Yankee. The public accusations of Rodell Carney and Clint Stokes were completely unfair. To add to his gloom, the weather turned foul.

The crowded prisoners were exposed to the worst of the winter gales, with only bits of old canvas to protect them as they huddled together on the open deck.

Captain Semmes fought the winds and adverse currents for several days with both steam and sails, but it was too great a strain on the precious coal supply. Under canvas alone, the cruiser made little headway.

Nine harrowing days and nights passed before the cruiser made the west end of Jamaica.

The harbor of Port Royal was free of the storm winds. Sailors, prisoners and officers relaxed from the dreadful discomforts they had suffered. Permission was granted by the English authorities to land the prisoners, and they were paroled.

A friend invited Captain Semmes to his home in the country for a brief rest, and he left Lieutenant Kell in command of the ship.

The executive officer was an efficient disciplinarian, but the long voyage without liberty was too much for many of the crew. This was a gay port and they made the most of it. After Kell had been forced to send the cutters and shore boats in, time after time, for the crew members who had overstayed their liberties, he refused to permit any more men to go ashore.

Natives in dugouts were constantly alongside the ship, selling fruit, flowers and examples of basketwork and primitive jewelry. A couple of sailors, feeling abused at having been dragged back from liberty, dived overboard, jumped into a dugout and seized the paddles from the native owners. They shoved out in haste and headed for shore.

Lieutenant Kell, his usual calm broken by sleepless nights, angrily ordered Tim and five oarsmen to give chase in one of the cruiser's boats.

The two sailors in the dugout were at a great disadvantage against the five rowers in the sleek cutter. Just as Tim and his men grew close, he heard one of the fleeing sailors say, "I'll tell you what the trouble is, Bill. There's too much cargo in this craft, and I'm going to lighten ship a little."

With that, he grabbed one of the natives and pitched him overboard! Port Royal Bay was full of sharks; Tim couldn't abandon the terrified native.

One of Tim's oarsmen reached for the floundering man, but missed. The cutter had to turn about to complete the rescue. The delay had given the dugout added yards, but Tim urged his oarsmen to greater speed.

Just as he was about to overtake the little boat, the sailors tossed the other native into the water.

Back on the deck of the *Alabama,* officers and crew crowded the rails to watch the race in the moonlight. Cheers and laughter floated over the calm waters and even in his annoyance, Tim had to chuckle. This chase was fun!

The cutter scooped up the second victim and went on to capture the runaways. The sailors, beaten fairly in the race and completely out-of-breath from their efforts, were meek now.

The natives were restored to their own boat, and the sailors taken on board the cutter.

Lieutenant Kell sent an urgent message to Captain Semmes, asking him to return.

A few minutes after a stern-faced Captain Semmes had stepped aboard, he summoned Armstrong, Maffitt, Stokes and Moore to his cabin.

The young officers stepped lively. "Wonder what we've done wrong?" Maffitt muttered to Tim.

Tim shrugged, but he looked worried.

"Gentlemen," Captain Semmes greeted them grimly, "it seems there has been a serious breach of discipline during my absence. The conduct of the crew is disgraceful, of course. The most flagrant conduct, however, has been the brawling on shore of one of our own Confederate officers.

"The paymaster has been absent from his duties for 3 days and 3 nights. It will be difficult to restore order at best, but it would be well-nigh impossible if the crew were aware of his delinquency. I want you to go ashore at once, find him, and bring him back quietly after dark. I wish this scandal to be kept from the crew."

Tim, since Rodell Carney and Clint Stokes had accused him so unfairly of being friendly to the Yankees, had avoided the wardroom at times when he thought they might be there. The captain's remarks came to him as a complete surprise, but most of the others seemed to know of Carney's absence from the ship.

Still, all were shocked when they found the paymaster. He was in the fifth and worst of the saloons they searched. His uniform was dirty, his waxed mustache drooping, his hair uncombed. He was humped, half-asleep, over a half-empty bottle and an empty glass.

Maffitt and Armstrong roused him, each tugging at an arm and pulling him to his feet. His eyes opened and he fixed Tim with a baleful look. "What are you doing, sneaking around spying on me? Why aren't you hobnobbing with some of your Yankee friends you pulled out of the briny? Still plenty of 'em on shore here and they'd be glad to buy you a drink."

"Sir, Captain Semmes has asked us to bring you on board," Tim replied, carefully keeping his voice level.

With an effort, the man tried to stand more erectly. "So, the old rascal came back early from his holiday, did he? Well, I'll just have to have a little talk with him."

Stokes whispered to Armstrong, "It's still an hour until it's dark enough to take him on board. Suppose we could find some place to douse his head in cold water and clean him up? None of the crew is on shore and there'd be no danger whatsoever of them seeing him."

"The British would," the older officer objected swiftly. "I wouldn't want them to see our uniform disgraced this way. I'll try to get some coffee here in this hole, and we'll wait until dark to get him out in the street."

Carney refused the coffee and tried instead to pour another drink from his bottle. In disgust, Armstrong knocked the bottle from the table to the filthy floor. Carney was wrathful, but Maffitt and Armstrong held him on the bench by sheer force.

Tim thought the hour would never end. Carney swore, raged, sneered. Even though the man had been unfair to him, Tim took no joy in the situation. The paymaster was a Confederate officer on a proud ship, and his conduct disgraced all his fellow shipmates.

At last it was dark and they made their way down side streets to the wharf, literally dragging Carney along.

"Semmes will throw him in chains, if he sees him in this shape," Stokes said to Tim, as they followed the others.

"I've never seen the captain so angry," Tim agreed.

"If Carney just had a chance to sober up and clean up—and the captain had time to simmer down—it still might be possible to save him," Stokes went on eagerly. "Are you willing to try to help him escape? Just temporarily, of course."

"Jiminy, no!" Tim burst out indignantly. "Our orders were to bring him in."

"You've always hated Carney, haven't you?" Stokes was speaking in a low, intense voice, so it wouldn't carry to the others a few steps ahead. "You're plumb happy to find him this way, aren't you?"

Tim started to deny the charge, then shrugged. He must learn to hold his tongue, and nothing he could say would change Stokes' opinion.

Carney's punishment was more severe and final than a week in chains.

No one ever knew what Captain Semmes said to the paymaster, but a half hour after the boat had reached the *Alabama* with Carney, the same four officers who'd brought him from shore were taking him back. It was difficult to recognize the dapper officer now. He was in rumpled old civilian clothes and carried a single valise. He'd been stripped of uniform and rank and was being put off the cruiser forever.

Only Stokes shook hands with him and murmured a few words, before the four young men silently rowed back to their ship.

Chapter 10

LONG CRUISE

LATE in January Tim was on duty when Lieutenant Kell sent him below to inspect the hold. It was one of his daily chores. The executive officer had explained early in the cruise, "Fire at sea is always a dreadful threat, but in a ship-of-war with loaded magazines and shell rooms, it is doubly dangerous. Any careful senior officer will have the hold checked during every watch."

It had become so much of a routine after all these months that Tim's inspection took only a few minutes. Rather absently, he covered his usual trail, checking by sniffing almost as much as he did by sight in the dim light.

Tim was thinking to himself how much more pleasant the *Alabama* seemed with Carney gone. Of course, Stokes continued his complaining and jeering and talking about wanting to go home.

Tim stepped above into the clear, crisp sunshine on deck and reported, "All correct, sir," to his senior officer.

It was only a matter of moments before the dread cry sounded. "Fire!"

Aghast, Tim stared at Lieutenant Kell. The shout had come from the hold. Lieutenant Kell ordered the drummer to beat to quarters and followed Tim as he ran toward the cry.

Tim, in the dusky hold, could see a midshipman beating at a blaze near the grog room with his uniform jacket. Tim tore off his own and flailed at the flames.

Seconds later the fire was smothered, but Lieutenant Kell ordered a sailor to stand by with two buckets of water, in case a spark had been missed.

Tim, brows scorched, ruefully picked up his ruined coat. Only then did he realize the other midshipman was Clint Stokes. "That was lucky," he said. "How'd you happen by in such good season?"

"I was just going by the hatch and thought I smelled smoke."

Lieutenant Kell, his face stern, said, "Mr. Moore, it hasn't been 10 minutes since your inspection. What is your explanation?"

Tim swallowed hard before replying. It had been just that long ago that he'd thought his troubles were over, because Carney was no longer aboard! "There wasn't a sign of smoke or fire when I was below," he said. "I checked here and then the magazine and shell rooms, just as I always do."

"You didn't happen to light a candle for your inspection, did you?" Stokes asked. "I thought I could smell burning tallow."

"No, of course I didn't. It's against orders." Tim was indignant at the suggestion. "I'm not that big a fool!"

"That will do, gentlemen." Lieutenant Kell's tone was icy. "Hereafter, Mr. Moore, I will assume the responsibility of checking for fire. Mr. Stokes, I wish to congratulate you on being so swift to act in this danger. I shall see that your quick thinking is brought to the attention of Captain Semmes and the other officers."

Again, Tim spent many miserable and sleepless

nights. There hadn't been any smoke in the hold when he inspected. He hadn't used a candle or lantern. There had been no signs of any other crew member about. No one—except Stokes.

Shuddering, Tim rejected this frightful idea. He wouldn't be such an idiot as to start that fire, just to make me look careless and stupid and to make himself a hero.

Tim grimly and resolutely carried out his duties, but it was a dull and disappointing part of the cruise.

The weeks passed uneventfully.

"Old Semmes must be losing his touch," Stokes remarked to Tim one night as they were turning in after a watch. "Pretty silly, really. Only four captures in 3 months."

Tim stared at Stokes. Ever since Carney had been thrown off the ship, Stokes had been grumbling. Even he, however, had never gone so far as to criticize Captain Semmes before. Tim suspected part of it was that the grousing midshipman had had to stand the usual night watches, now that he was no longer assistant to the paymaster.

"Just not as many Union sails in sight," Tim replied at last. "Even the Union newspapers we've captured have been full of the news of Yankee skippers selling to neutrals at losses."

Stokes scowled. "Just the same, we won't catch any ships off Brazil. It's a poor place to hunt."

"We're here to meet the *Agrippina* for fresh supplies and coal. She's already 10 days late. If the supply ship doesn't turn up from England by tomorrow, we're going to start transferring from that last capture, the *Louisa Hatch*. She's loaded with coal, worth seventeen dollars a ton."

"Trust you to know all the answers," Stokes sneered. "Pays off for you to be around the top officers."

Tim held back a wrathful retort. It was useless to argue with Stokes when he was in one of his frequent black moods.

After the transfer of coal, a new cruise was set for the *Alabama*.

She'd been operating off the coast of Brazil for several weeks, and the enemy had had plenty of time to send Union men-of-war in pursuit.

Then disaster struck! Weevil had destroyed almost all the supply of bread! Since it was impossible to face a long trip without bread, Captain Semmes had to give orders to put back to Rio de Janeiro, more than 800 miles away, for a new supply.

The weather was foul and oppressive. During this time, eleven ships were intercepted and chased. All were neutral.

The raider still persisted in chasing every sail and on the 1st of July, the *Anna F. Schmidt* was captured.

Tim was in the boarding party and could scarcely wait to get back with the news. He raced to the captain's cabin.

"Sir!" he announced breathlessly, "we found a 30-day supply of bread in airtight casks."

Captain Semmes gave Tim one of his rare, warm smiles and promptly ordered the cruiser put about.

For several weeks, the cruiser was out of the world trade routes. In almost 1,000 miles, only one ship was sighted.

Finally, the *Alabama* put in at Saldanha Bay, a beautiful landlocked smooth anchorage, sheltered from the wind and within a few hours of the Cape of Good Hope, the halfway mark between extreme east and west.

Machinery, hull and rigging of the cruiser needed overhauling. Recaulking inside and out and repainting were necessary.

Captain Semmes reported to his officers, "You will all be relieved to know that the coal merchants at Cape Town have agreed to supply us. It has been a great worry. I left urgent messages at both Fernando de Noronha and Bahia for the *Agrippina* to meet us here. She should have been ahead of us by several weeks."

The ship at last doubled the Cape of Good Hope, with its headland and lighthouse perched hundreds of feet above the black rocks.

When the fresh stores were aboard, Captain Semmes made known his plans for the future. "We're to make a long cruise on to the East Indies." The men took the news in solemn silence. It would be months before they returned to the Cape.

During most of September and October, the main

topic of interest was the cruiser's speed. She averaged 180 miles a day.

Since the coal supply was low after the long trip across the Indian Ocean, Captain Semmes was obliged to use sails most of the time. The sea was so shallow the ship anchored at night and navigated only in daylight.

Tim had the watch on the run to Singapore and was delighted to report to his superiors: "There are twenty-two Union ships, large Indiamen, almost all dismantled."

Captain Semmes' iron-gray brows seemed to bristle more than ever, but there was a sparkle in his eyes. "The Yankee flag is becoming a stranger to the China Seas," he said in satisfaction. "The masters are safe here in Singapore. The few who are brave enough to risk their ships cannot find owners willing to risk their cargoes."

The *Alabama* filled her coal bunkers and returned to raiding duties after a brief stay in port.

Tim's second Christmas away from home passed quietly. He tried desperately not to think of his home so far away in Virginia, or of his family, from whom he'd had no news in more than 18 months.

The last day of 1863 found the raider leaving the coast of Sumatra. She set an easy sail along the wide waters toward the east coast of Africa. The weather was delightful, and for 12 days and nights not even a studding sail was lowered.

Tim was aching for some fun, and the countless schools of flying fish gave him an idea. He enlisted the aid of the ship's carpenter.

The officers and crew, having little to do in this easy sailing weather, gathered to watch. They lined the rails, jeering and chuckling, but curious. Tim spread a net with outriggers, just under the bow of the ship.

"Trying to catch a mermaid?"

"Naw. Anyone can see he's going to capture old Father Neptune."

Tim, grinning, ignored the remarks.

Finally, it was night. The darkness was black, velvety, almost solid enough to touch. Tim, paying no attention to the noisy watchers lining the rails, lowered a ship's lantern on a rope, holding it just above the net. For a long while, nothing happened.

There were catcalls, hoots, jokes from all hands. Tim, still silent, held the rope with a steady hand. Suddenly, a whole cloud of flying fish rose to the bait of the lighted lantern. The fish rushed at the light, struck the bow of the ship and fell to the net beneath.

The watchers became quiet. Ten minutes later, another whole school of flying fish was caught. In an hour's time, the net contained hundreds. Every man on board was assured all the fresh fish he could eat for breakfast.

The *Alabama* ran in to Cape Town on the 20th of March, almost 6 months from the September day they had left.

The night after leaving the Cape, Captain Semmes kept his officers at table.

"I was so occupied with business and guests at the Cape, I didn't have time to read the papers which our friends brought. Gentlemen, the news is not encouraging.

"Although we seem to have succeeded in our own mission of sweeping the seas of enemy commerce, our people at home are being harder and harder pressed.

"The Union blockade is more effective all along the coast. The signs of weakness which first became apparent when we lost at Gettysburg and Vicksburg last July are multiplying."

He sighed, and the men around the table waited in grim attentiveness. "I propose to put in a neutral port, probably in France, to seek a dry dock. We will, of course, continue to seek out the enemy on the way and destroy him where we find him.

"Please keep this conversation in confidence. We will be at sea for several weeks, and there is no need for this word to spread among the crew."

Chapter 11

CHALLENGE

NOT until late April did the *Alabama* make another capture. She was the *Rockingham*. The chase took all night, and it was clearly evident the Confederate raider was in serious need of repairs.

The boilers were burned out and the machinery faulty. Seams were open, and the copper on her bottom was in rolls or missing.

"It took us twice as long as it should have to make that capture." Lieutenant Kell's tone was grim. "We'll use her for some much-needed target practice, as soon as the cargo and prisoners are on board us."

Tim nodded. "Shall I alert the gun crews?"

"Shouldn't be more than a half hour. I've told the boarding party not to fire her."

It took several hours to sink the captured merchant vessel because, although the range was accurate, the powder was faulty.

Captain Semmes and Lieutenant Kell watched the

performance in silence. Tim, at his station next to the executive officer, waited anxiously for some comment.

"The powder has been stored for 20 months," Lieutenant Kell said.

"It has deteriorated badly." Captain Semmes straightened his shoulders. "One good thing—we aren't likely to run into an enemy man-of-war. This settles it; we must get on to a neutral port without delay."

Tim turned away. He bumped awkwardly into Stokes, who had an odd grin on his face. "Can't you see where you're going, Mr. Moore?" There was no malice, only cheerfulness in his tone.

"Sorry," Tim blurted.

Why was Stokes so pleasant, all of a sudden?

At noon on June 11, the *Alabama* dropped anchor in the port of Cherbourg, France.

Permission was obtained from the port admiral to land the prisoners from the last two captures.

All the docks at Cherbourg belonged to the French Government, and the local official felt he hadn't the authority to permit their use by a belligerent ship. It was decided to ask the Emperor himself to answer the request.

Word was sent by telegraph to Paris. In a few hours the reply came that Napoleon III was enjoying a brief holiday at Biarritz and would answer on his return to Paris. There was nothing to do but wait.

Three days later the U. S. S. *Kearsarge* steamed into the harbor. The men on the raider lined the rails to watch, in tense excitement.

The enemy sent a boat ashore to communicate with authorities. She didn't anchor, but again steamed out and took a station outside the breakwater.

The Union ship, it was quickly learned, had arrived to pick up the prisoners released from the raider.

Captain Semmes immediately objected on the ground that the enemy would be adding to her crew while she was in neutral territory. The French officials agreed.

Captain Semmes called a council in his cabin. "I am going out to fight the *Kearsarge*. What do you think of it?"

His words were greeted with cheers. Gravely, the leader held up his hand for silence. "It has been difficult for you—trained, courageous men—as it has been for me, to accept the taunts of our enemies. For almost 2 years, they've termed us heartless bullies who have never taken on anything our size, but have only preyed on helpless merchantmen."

His voice and eyes were stern. "Our task, to clear our foes' trade from the seas, has been successfully performed.

"As to the *Kearsarge,* we're evenly matched. We have one more gun, but their 11-inchers may be more effective at short range. They are rumored to have a dozen more men in their crew than our 149."

The meeting ended in patriotic enthusiasm for the battle ahead.

Captain Semmes wrote a message of challenge to his French agent, to be delivered to the enemy counsel and forwarded to Capt. John A. Winslow of the *Kearsarge.*

C.S.S. *Alabama,* Cherbourg, June 14, 1864

To A. Bonfils, Esq., Cherbourg.

Sir: I hear that you were informed by the United States consul that the *Kearsarge* was to come to this port solely for the prisoners landed by me, and that she was to depart in twenty-four hours. I desire you to say to the United States consul that my intention is to fight the *Kearsarge* as soon as I can make the necessary arrangements. I hope these will not detain me more than until tomorrow evening, or after the morrow morning at the furthest. I beg she will not depart before I am ready to go out.

I have the honor to be, very respectfully,

Your obedient servant,

R. Semmes, Captain.

The answer came promptly, through the channels of the commercial agents on shore.

Captain Winslow didn't reply in writing. He snorted indignantly that he had come to Cherbourg to fight.

There were signs of feverish activity on both ships. The *Alabama,* coal bunkers filled, was scrubbed and polished. In spite of working the clock around, it was not until Saturday evening, June 18, that the preparations were complete.

Captain Semmes notified the port admiral of his intention to sail out of harbor the next morning. The messenger returned with word that the French ironclad frigate *Couronne* would accompany the raider, to see that the neutrality of their waters would not be violated.

Sunday dawned bright and clear. It seemed as if all of Europe had been alerted to the coming duel. Excursion trains had come from Paris, carrying gay holiday crowds, to watch the battle. These, along with French people from the town and neighboring villages, filled the heights above the harbor, every window with a view of the sea, and the walls and fortifications of the harbor.

French fishing boats and even an English pleasure yacht, the *Deerhound,* went outside the harbor to view the well-publicized fight.

Officers and crew alike on board the raider were lighthearted. It was Midshipman Anderson who had pointed out at breakfast that Sunday was the raider's lucky day. "Captain Semmes assumed command, we were commissioned and we flew our Confederate flag for the first time on Sundays. We captured the *Ariel* and sank the *Hatteras* on that day of the week, also."

As the British members of the crew stepped smartly

to their tasks, they sang a new song, composed by Sam Storr, for the occasion.

"We're homeward bound; we're homeward bound
And soon shall stand on English ground.
But ere that English land we see
We first must fight the Kear—sar—geeee!"

That morning, the sea was as calm as a bowl of water. Tim's heart swelled with pride as he saw the cruiser, decks fresh and clean, brasswork shining in the sun, and the beloved Confederate flag at the mast. Everyone aboard was wearing his best uniform.

Crowds clustered on the breakwater broke into cheers and waved as the sleek cruiser steamed through the western entrance of the harbor, the French iron-clad following. Trailing at a safe distance were the fishing boats and the English yacht.

Tim, at his familiar station near Lieutenant Kell, had a good view of the enemy ship about 7 miles out.

The French ship anchored just outside the breakwater.

It would take about three-quarters of an hour to run out to the *Kearsarge,* and it was almost a leisurely manner in which the orders to quarters, to cast loose the battery, were repeated through the executive officer's trumpet.

Previously the yards had been slung in chains,

stoppers prepared for the rigging. Now the magazine and shell rooms were opened, the decks sanded down, the tubs filled with water. Gun crews stripped to the waist.

The order came for officers and crew to come aft. Not since the raider had been commissioned, so many action-filled months before, had Captain Semmes addressed all of his men.

The officer had put on formal dress, his frock-coated uniform with three rows of gleaming buttons, gold-braid epaulettes, and sword. He stood erectly on the horse block, a platform just forward of the mizzen-mast.

Tim thrilled to his words.

"Officers and seamen of the *Alabama!* You have, at length, another opportunity of meeting the enemy—the first that has been presented to you since you sank the *Hatteras*.

"In the meantime, you have been all over the world, and it is not too much to say that you have destroyed, and driven for protection under neutral flags, one-half the enemy's commerce, which at the beginning of the war covered every sea.

"This is an achievement of which you may well be proud; and a grateful country will not be unmindful of it.

"The name of your ship has become a household word wherever civilization extends. Shall that name be tarnished by defeat? The thing is impossible!

"Remember you are in the English Channel, the theater of so much of the naval glory of our race, and the eyes of all Europe are at this moment upon you.

"The flag that floats over you is that of a young Republic, who bids defiance to her enemies, whenever and wherever found. Show the world that you know how to uphold it.

"Go to your quarters."

With the third broadside from the Confederate ship, the enemy sheered, and answering fire came at last from her entire starboard battery.

"She's going to try to run under our stern!" Tim shouted in excitement.

His voice was unheard in the din of the firing. Semmes and Kell had foreseen the maneuver. The *Alabama* was sheering, too. Thus, the pattern of the great battle was set.

Now the ships were circling around a common center, the distance between them varying from a half to a quarter of a mile.

Later on, Tim was never able to remember the consecutive scenes of the next few frantic hours.

Captain Semmes, still standing fearlessly on the horse block forward the mizzenmast, observed through his glasses the effect of their fire. Tim, having just given him a message from Lieutenant Kell, was given one in return. "Tell Mr. Kell to use solid shot." His tone was puzzled. "Our shells strike the enemy's side and fall into the water."

Tim raced with the message and the executive officer gave the order to the gun crews. Solid shot appeared ineffective also, so alternate shot and shell were tried.

The fire from the enemy was doing fearful damage. Their 11-inch shells were hitting the quarterdeck section in terrifying regularity. Three of them in a few minutes entered the port of the 8-inch pivot gun.

The first shell swept off the forward part of the gun's crew. The second killed one man instantly and seriously wounded three others. The third struck the breast of the gun carriage and spun it around on the deck. Almost automatically, several men lifted it and threw it overboard.

In the midst of the noise, smoke and confusion, the veteran captain took note of the damage to the *Kearsarge.*

One of the *Alabama*'s 68-pounders went through the bulwarks of the enemy ship and exploded on the quarterdeck. Two shots entered the ports of the 30-pounders. A shell exploded in the hammock nettings and set fire, but it was quickly put out.

The Union ship kept her sights lowered, and her guns hammered away at the water line of the raider. The latter was careening heavily to starboard.

During the entire action, both ships maintained a strong port helm and seven complete circles were made.

Now the decks were slippery with blood, in spite of the liberal sprinkling of sand.

The most painful command Tim had to relay from Lieutenant Kell was to order the men to throw the mangled bodies overboard. The port side of the quarterdeck was so littered it would have been impossible to fight the after pivot gun unless this brutal duty was completed.

The heroic fighters went to their watery graves without the rites they had earned so gallantly.

A 100-pound shell from the *Alabama*'s Blakely gun penetrated the stern of the *Kearsarge,* lodging in the sternpost. Semmes could see the vessel trembling from bowsprit to rudder at the shock.

The shell failed to explode!

It was a bitter blow for the Confederates. Had the large shell burst in such a vital spot, victory would have been in the *Alabama*'s grasp within minutes.

It was then Captain Semmes gave the order to make

all headway possible when the circuit of fight should put the bow of his cruiser toward the coast. The maneuver was to pivot to port and continue the action with the port battery, while trying to reach the safe neutral waters.

It was too late. The engineer, his face haggard and streaked, came on deck to report his fires were put out. He could no longer work the engines.

The captain gave the order to Lieutenant Kell. "Go below, sir, and see how long the ship can float."

Tim raced with him. The familiar wardroom was unrecognizable. The assistant surgeon stood at his post, but the table and patient upon it had been swept away from him by an 11-inch shell which had opened the side of the ship. Already the deck was awash.

"We needn't check any more," Lieutenant Kell said, his face white and his voice a whisper.

Tim listened, still unbelieving, as the officer made his report to the captain that the cruiser would sink in a matter of minutes.

"Then, sir, cease firing. Haul down the colors."

Abruptly, there were only the screams and moans of the wounded to break the silence.

The dinghy and one slightly damaged quarterboat were lowered with the wounded. Dr. Galt was given the sad duty of taking them to the *Kearsarge*.

Tim was sobbing shamelessly when the last dread order came.

Lieutenant Kell had difficulty in keeping his voice

steady as he shouted, "Everybody overboard! Abandon ship! Take a spar and save yourselves!"

Even with the direct command, many of the men refused to believe that the sturdy *Alabama* could be in her last struggle. Kell hurried forward, urging the men to jump.

The decks were swiftly cleared, save for the dead.

Captain Semmes put on a life preserver and Lieutenant Kell seized a wooden grating.

Without a word to his men, the captain strode to the rail and threw his cherished sword into the sea.

Tim took a last look at the splintered, blood-stained deck, slipped off his shoes, and dove cleanly over the rail. The water was full of empty shell cases and bobbing, sputtering heads,

Tim swam away from the doomed ship, but turned once to look over his shoulder. The *Alabama,* graceful to the last, was settling swiftly at the stern. Water had entered the berth deck ports, and was forcing the air upward in a huge sigh. The shattered mainmast broke and fell. The guns and everything loose on the decks thundered aft, forcing the bow high in the air as she made the final plunge.

Now Tim looked around to see if any of his shipmates needed aid. One dark-haired man nearby was in trouble. He'd seized a spar, but was struggling violently, floundering and swallowing water.

Tim swam closer. "Quit fighting," he ordered. "Just float with the spar until you get your breath."

It was Stokes, his face in a grimace of terror. He clutched at Tim, letting go the spar.

Tim knew the blind panic that seized people helpless in the water. He wriggled out of Stokes' grip, thrust the spar between them. "Hang on to it," he shouted sternly, "and I'll tow you to a boat."

He looked around. Only 20 yards to the right was a rescue boat from the *Kearsarge*. About 80 yards to his left was a boat from the English yacht.

Tim was faced with the most difficult decision of his life. If he abandoned Stokes, he could swim to the English boat and to freedom, to fight again for his beloved Confederacy!

He couldn't tow Stokes that far; he couldn't let him drown either.

It had to be the Yankee boat. Now, he thought bitterly, I'll be a prisoner for the rest of the war.

The blue-clad sailors fished them out of the water, pushed them toward the stern and went on with the rescue work.

Tim flopped alongside Lieutenant Sinclair. He breathed deeply a few moments, then pulled himself up to look about. The boat from the English yacht had drifted a little nearer.

With renewed hope, he whispered to Stokes and Sinclair, "We can make it to that boat." He nodded in the direction. "It's an easy swim and the Yankees forward are too busy to miss us."

Sinclair sat up, his expression cheerful. "Why not try?"

"Between us, we can get you there," Tim said, turning to Stokes.

He was still struggling to catch his breath. "I'm where I want to be . . . you can't do anything about it. . . . I'll even tell you we rigged that fake count on the stores at the beginning of the cruise. . . . I set that fire to make you look bad, to get even with you for not helping me with Carney."

Tim, in a terrible rage, started to jerk Stokes to his feet.

Sinclair pulled Tim back. "Not now. Not if we want to get free."

Stokes managed a faint smirk. "I am grateful to you, Tim, for saving my life. If you want to try it, I'll not give the alarm. It would have been fun for me, though, to be a midshipman on the *Kearsarge* and you a prisoner."

Tim nodded to Sinclair and they slid over the stern.

Fortunately, the boat from the yacht was still headed their way and still rescuing men from the water.

Tim, swimming steadily alongside Sinclair, was shocked at Clint Stokes' confession. He had been both blind and stupid not to see that Carney and Stokes were traitors. Clint's words echoed, *"I'm where I want to be."*

Maybe sometime he'd have the chance to tell Captain Semmes and Lieutenant Kell the truth about the inventory and the fire.

Tim chuckled suddenly and swallowed salt water. Sputtering, but not losing the rhythm of his stroke, he thought, But I'm where I want to be, too. All I've wanted for 3 years is to fight for the Confederacy. Now, I'll have a chance to fight again.

A few minutes later a rope was tossed from the boat and Tim and Sinclair seized it eagerly. They were pulled aboard, really exhausted now, to find Captain Semmes stretched out in the stern sheets and pale as death. He had a slightly wounded arm and was weakened from his ordeal in the water.

Minutes later, they were on board the *Deerhound*. Her boats had picked up forty of the *Alabama*'s survivors.

The rescued were crowded together on the deck of the pleasure yacht. Mr. Lancaster, the owner, and his crew went among them, serving hot tea laced with rum. This, and the hot sun, soon revived the chilled, exhausted men.

Tim overheard Captain Semmes expressing his gratitude to the Englishman.

"You really owe your rescue to my 9-year-old daughter, Catherine," he replied. "I had been on the Continent and had ordered my captain to pick me up in Cherbourg. My wife, three sons, daughter and niece were aboard. I had intended to take them to church this morning, but the boys wanted to see the fight. The vote was evenly divided until Catherine sided with her brothers."

Later, the barefoot, wet, bedraggled men gathered around their captain, who had asked Lieutenant Kell to get their attention.

"Men, we can be grateful that we are alive. And still free! We made an honorable fight. We must not dwell too long and mournfully on our loss. The good and courageous companions of almost 2 years would not want us to lose heart now.

"Lieutenant Kell has told me that our powder was faulty. It is not surprising, since we have been cruising in all climates with it during the last 22 months. I saw one of our shells make a direct hit on their sternpost during the battle, which would have put them out of the fight if it had exploded." His pale face was stern as he went on. "Not only that, I have learned why neither solid shot nor shell seemed to have any effect. The *Kearsarge* was wearing a coat of mail. Her chain cable was hung vertically on her sides, covered with deal boards."

He turned to ease the pain in his arm. "There was no time to tell you, during the preparations for battle, that I had some bad news from our agent ashore in Cherbourg. It is now no mystery why our supply ship failed us during more than a year of the latter part of our cruise. He was paid well not to come to our aid. It is a bitter thing to know that a man wearing our honored uniform could be a traitor."

The men looked puzzled. Surely that old Scots captain was never in the Confederacy!

Semmes managed a slight smile. "I mean Carney, of course. He is now operating in London, openly working for the Yankees. He is the one who paid off the old captain of the supply ship."

Tim almost stepped forward to say that Stokes had tried to keep Carney on the *Alabama* and that just a few minutes before, aboard the rescue boat from the Union ship, Stokes had said, "I'm where I want to be."

This was no time for accusations or for personal

revenge. Later he could clear his own record of the clouds of the inventory and the fire.

Tim was quiet as he straightened proudly and heard the captain's next words.

"We've earned a brief holiday, which we shall have in England. Our deeds on the *Alabama* will live long in history. I give you my word that as soon as possible we shall return to our beloved homeland, where we will be together again and fight for our glorious Confederacy."

Epilogue

Captain Raphael Semmes, after recuperating in England, made a long, difficult and secret return to the South. He became rear admiral of the Confederacy in 1865, charged with the defense of Richmond. When that city was captured, he blew up his ships in the James River, and with his men joined the army of General Johnston. He had the unusual distinction of being both a rear admiral and a brigadier general.

After the war, he practiced law in Mobile, Alabama, and wrote a number of books concerning his military experiences.

Although the cruise of the *Alabama* lasted less than 2 years, the conflict over her lasted a decade. The *Florida* and the *Shenandoah,* other Confederate raiders, were also built in England. These ships caused great damage to the Union merchant marine.

At the end of the war, the United States claimed damages from England, because the three ships had been built, fitted out and otherwise aided by English interests.

In 1871 and again in 1872, five men met to arbitrate the "*Alabama* Claims" in Geneva. There were representatives from England, the United States, and three neutral countries, Italy, Switzerland and Brazil. The tribunal decided to set a sum in gross for all direct damages, and England paid the United States $15,500,000 in gold.